417947

W
Bla

417947

TRAIL OF WHITENED SKULLS

TRAIL OF WHITENED SKULLS

SKULLS

The Cole Lavery Saga

Tom W. Blackburn

Five Star • Waterville, Maine

First Edition
First Printing: September, 2006

Published in 2006 in conjunction with Golden West Literary Agency.

Set in 11 pt. Plantin.

Printed in the United States on permanent paper.

Library of Congress Cataloging-in-Publication Data

Blackburn, Thomas Wakefield.
    Trail of whitened skulls : the Cole Lavery saga / by Tom W. Blackburn.—1st ed.
      p. cm.
     ISBN 1-59414-395-1 (hc : alk. paper)
     1. Western stories.   I. Title.
PS3552.L3422T73 2006
 813'.54—dc22   2006012778

TRAIL OF WHITENED SKULLS

Table of Contents

Foreword

by
Jon Tuska

Thomas Wakefield Blackburn was born on the T.O. Ranch near Raton, New Mexico, on June 23, 1913. His father, Howard Blackburn, was employed at the time by the O'Shaunnessy Engineering Company and had been transferred to the T.O. Ranch to design an irrigation system and see it installed. He had recently married Edith Herrington of LaSalle, Colorado, and brought his wife to stay with him on the ranch. That is how Tom, the eldest of six children, came to be born there. Later Tom would include this ranch—which controlled such a vast domain that it even had its own internal railroad system—in his novel, *Raton Pass* (Doubleday, 1950).

Blackburn's mother carried on the tradition of coining diminutive nicknames for family members—hers was "Didi", which she was first called by her parents—and Tom was familiarly known as "Wakey" through high school. When the irrigation job was completed, Howard Blackburn returned to LaSalle. Howard took over the farm where Edith's father had been living because his job with the Union Pacific had required him to move from LaSalle to Pierce, a nearby town smaller than LaSalle. Being a slight man (one-half inch over five feet and weighing 135 pounds), Howard was simply not cut out for farming. When the Great War came, Howard worked for a contractor who was buying dry-farmed navy beans grown in the arid land known as the sand hills in eastern Colorado and that were to be sold to the Armed Services. This job was not much of an improvement on farming and, by the war's end, Howard was back in LaSalle where he held a succession of jobs, including that of town marshal.

Finally, with financial help from his father, Howard opened a Ford Motors agency in LaSalle that was not particularly successful. However, success did come at last when, after additional assistance from his father, Howard went to Denver and enrolled in an insurance program at Denver University, commuting between the two cities. Upon completion of the program, he was hired as an assistant manager by the Federal Surety Company and worked out of the Denver office. Tom was in the fourth grade when his family took up permanent residence in Denver. By the time Howard became manager of the Denver office, he was making use of his engineering background supervising the completion of construction jobs where the company had bonded the original contractors and they were, for various reasons, unable to finish a particular job. Young Tom, rather than being allowed his freedom in the summer, accompanied his father from one construction camp to another where he was assigned a variety of jobs, from sitting in the barrow pit of a steam shovel counting with a mechanical hand counter the number of truck loads of fill processed on a given day to helping operate a camp store and cranking a bellows for the camp blacksmith. Tom also was asked by his young Uncle Cecil to help him with his wholesale produce business that consisted of driving his truck around to various ranches in the area and buying truck loads of fresh vegetables. For a time Howard moved the family to Lander, Wyoming, where he rented a large home while he supervised a highway construction project. The house was so big that Didi engaged a maid who was an Arapaho and a graduate of the Indian school at Ethete where the Arapahos had a combined reservation with the Shoshones. In English her name was Martha and in Arapaho, Agnowaneese, literally "painted woman" because of a large purple birthmark on her cheek. She remained with the family until Howard moved from Denver to Glendale, California.

Among his literary mentors Blackburn was wont to mention Didi first. For many years in addition to raising a family she wrote juvenile poetry for Sunday school magazines and pulp stories for the true confessions magazines. Once she was greatly embarrassed when a story she titled "Rosemary for Remembrance" appeared when published under the title "Six Weeks of Passion!" "Edith," said Howard, *"six weeks!"* When she was past sixty-five, she was still writing juvenile novels set in the early West that had gross sales exceeding the novels that by then her son was writing. Tom later recalled that "probably the most valuable thing she taught me was that writing was not necessarily for publication nor did it belong to any particular genre, that it was a profession somewhat similar to graphic arts in that you used a word as a vehicle for conveying a thought regardless of the means of presenting it."

Blackburn attended Glendale Junior College and then U.C.L.A. It was in Glendale that he met (Hazel) Juanita Alsdorf and they were married in that city on July 6, 1937. Tom and Juanita adopted Gary Keeling Blackburn, son of Juanita's sister, when he was orphaned. They also had two children of their own, Stephanie Blackburn, born

April 6, 1939, and Thomas Wakefield Blackburn III, born December 15, 1945. Tom would live long enough to know his grandson Thomas Wakefield Blackburn IV.

Tom turned to commercial writing after leaving college and presently became associated with writing syndicates headed by Harry F. Olmsted and Ed Earl Repp, the latter also a "B" Western screenwriter. These syndicates consisted of a pool of aspiring writers who were expected to ghost stories for Olmsted or Repp. It was believed that such stories would have a better chance for acceptance because of the high visibility of these authors with editors and readers. It is highly questionable if either Olmsted or Repp ever wrote any fiction that was not somehow a collaborative effort with another writer. Repp often used the Ann Elmo Literary Agency to circulate the stories his syndicate produced. Tom wrote numerous stories for Repp during 1937 and one for Olmsted. Olmsted, however, kept the original manuscripts of all the stories written for Repp as well as for himself. These manuscripts from numerous writers were destroyed in a fire in his study in 1939.

Many of the stories Tom W. Blackburn wrote for Repp were sold; some were not. When Tom saw Repp was able to send off the stories he wrote for publication without any editorial changes at all, he knew it was time for him to cast off on his own. He kept file cards for himself only on those stories to which Repp had contributed nothing. It was primarily to fill the vacancy that Blackburn's departure created that caused Repp to run the newspaper advertisement to which Frank Bonham replied. While Bonham hated for the rest of his life what he considered indentured servitude to Repp— even though it did allow him to establish his own career as a magazine writer—Blackburn was both grateful and cordial to Repp. On May 25, 1939 Blackburn wrote to Repp, giving him the titles to four stories he had sent to him, three from 1937 and the last one from May, 1938, which had not as yet found acceptance. Blackburn wanted the stories returned to him so that he could rework them. "I've run dryer than Chateau Yquem '88 and I might find something in them that would shape up under new handling."

Toward the end of 1939 Blackburn wrote again to Repp from the home he had taken in Santa Monica to tell him how delighted he was to watch the serial they had worked on together then running in *Wild West Weekly* and he announced proudly that he had a story under his own name in the current issue of *10 Story Western*. Unable to support himself and his family by writing alone, Blackburn went to work for the Gas Company and wrote to Repp that he sorely missed the days when he could happily make his living "pulpeteering". He had heard good things about Frank Bonham now and again and he confessed to Repp: **I am glad that you are not left stranded when I ran down. I should have felt very badly if you were. Our year of association was very pleasant and touched with a friendliness I should hate to lose**. By January, 1943, Blackburn's fortunes had improved. He was writing more and getting published more and he thanked Repp for the check he had sent him when the last of their collaborative stories had finally been accepted. On August 30, 1944 Blackburn wrote to Repp to tell him he did not **know if you are still trading a little first-class instruction in basic plot work for the efforts of an earnest beginner who wants very much to write Westerns. But in case you are, I know a lad up from Texas who may have enough on the ball to be of value to you**.

Occasionally Blackburn would avail himself of the services of Harlan Graves or William L. Hopson. Undistinguished writers themselves, they were the equivalent in writing fiction to a script doctor at a Hollywood studio who would be given an awkward script to polish. Olmstead got 75%, as did Repp, of what a story brought in for the use of his name. Graves and Hopson got sole credit in the byline but asked for only half the money. James Charles Lynch, who worked for Harry F. Olmsted's syndicate, became good friends with Blackburn and once in a while Tom would ask Jimmy to polish one his stories that had been rejected or Jimmy would ask the same of Tom. Their association outlasted this stage in their careers and later they would collaborate on screenplays or developing story ideas for producers.

Blackburn in growing up had lived at least briefly in a large number of small Western towns and had become fully acquainted with various members of these communities. "As a result," he later recalled, "I had a wide choice of activity and my trick—if indeed it was a trick—was to select out rather unique means of livelihood for my principal characters and hew to their trade pretty faithfully. So I wrote about blacksmiths and locksmiths and jewelers and occasionally bankers and newspaper editors (they were a favorite) and crew men on mining trains and sheepherders so that there was some variety to the stories."

What distinguishes Blackburn's early magazine fiction is the atmosphere of Greek drama where his protagonists are forced to come to terms with themselves and their past at a crucial moment of reckoning. For example, in "Epitaph for an Unmarked Grave" in *Star Western* (1/39), Kirk Brandon is the protagonist, a weathered man with years of success as head of a gang of cattle rustlers. Ernest Haycox was an obvious influence in the analogy of life with a poker game—which Haycox, in turn, had borrowed from Bret Harte, but

14

utilized in his own unique way. This analogy is an integral part of this story: "A strange deep glow was in Kirk Brandon's eyes. Many a lost-hope deal had come at last to the hands of this man who waited wisely and played his hand as his cards were dealt to him." Johnny Carter, who had once ridden with Brandon's gang, left him ten years before and married Molly Haskins with whom Kirk was in love at the same time. Brandon subsequently loaned Carter the money he needed to purchase the ranch he had been operating. Johnny is now dead, felled by an arrow from one of Cochise's renegade band. Kirk sends Molly Carter the notes for $10,000 that he held of Johnny's. He knows Molly loves the son she had with Johnny, who is now away at school. Kirk is hoping that Molly will be his. When she comes to see him at his hotel room, he is flushed by momentary enthusiasm. "For a moment Brandon believed he had won, hands elbow-high and without need of a showdown. But he soon saw he was wrong. Molly had never laid down a hand in her life and she intended to play this one." She agrees to become Kirk's wife and to go with him south to live across the border in a town she has always hated. As they are riding in a buckboard, Brandon begins to have second thoughts about his triumph, realizing that Molly's agreement has brought her great pain. They are beset by Indians. Brandon sends Molly back to Cordobal as he prepares to meet the Apaches alone. "Kirk Brandon stared after her for a fraction of a second with the sudden feeling that somehow the emptiness within him had been filled."

These early stories were extraordinary for their time and remain so. In "A Storm Comes to Crazy Horse" in *10 Story Western* (11/40), Bert White is the schoolteacher at Crazy Horse. He is in his shack when a terrible blizzard hits the district. Three hardcases, caught in the blizzard, come to his door and he invites them inside. Some time before his wife Lola had gone to Denver. On the stage ride back, the stage had been held up by Indian Yarrow and his gang and Lola, who was with child, had been shot to death. Now Indian Yarrow and two of his men are in Bert White's shack. Bert is an excellent teacher. His students would "bust their heads, learning from him, and they'd ride twenty miles of a Saturday, when there wasn't any school, to talk with him. They fed his soul, those kids, so that he couldn't die like he sometimes wanted. And he had to wait." Now, the waiting is over. The two gang members die as a result of exposure. Yarrow is in better shape. He takes off his boots, coat, and hat and tries to sleep on White's bed. Bert piles up all his possessions and then sets fire to them. Yarrow in a frenzy takes a shot at Bert and then escapes out into the blizzard with his clothes on fire. He is found the next day "face down—a madman caught in that frozen night without boots or jacket or cap." Bert is able in his final moments to sleep well.

"Three of a Kind—All Dead" in *10 Story Western* (7/42) is another fine story in the same vein with the protagonist an outlaw named Quint Dessalines. He and his bunch are being relentlessly pursued by a posse. These last hours of Dessalines's life are filled with memories of his own boyhood and sympathy is engendered for him. He manages to work it so that the youngest member of his gang escapes an ambush by lawmen and dies convinced that this time a running man is "headed in the right direction."

As Blackburn became more familiar with the needs and requirements of various editors at magazines, he increasingly tended to write to suit his markets. Evidently it was easier for him to write a straight action narrative with no probing of character and he could turn these out with greater speed than the kind of stories he had been writing previously. Both Alden Norton at *10 Story Western* and *Fifteen Western Tales* at Popular Publications and Harry Widmer, when he replaced Norton on *10 Story Western*, preferred stories that stressed action over character, while Mike Tilden, who replaced Rogers Terrill editing *Dime Western*, *Star Western*, and *New Western*, preferred stories that depended more on character than action. Blackburn, Bonham, and Lynch were among Tilden's favorite writers, and later Dan Cushman and Will Cook.

"The Fur Rebellion" in *10 Story Western* (10/43) has an interesting fur trade background but a routine plot of trappers and agents threatened by an aggressive take over by a German who wants to corner the market. The nationality of the villain, given the politics of the period, was not accidental. It wasn't too long before Tom began developing series characters for stories tailored to definite markets. Christian Defever, a former Shakespearean actor who was in his own words in "Boomer King of the Footlight Trail" in *10 Story Western* (4/44) " 'marooned by Fate' " because he once shot a man, was one of Blackburn's most popular series characters, based on the frequency with which stories about him appeared and the way their lengths were soon expanded from short stories to novelettes. The backgrounds developed around Defever are usually quite interesting, a mine collapse in this story, impersonating a famous trial lawyer in a complicated law case in "Chris Defever—Badlands Barrister" in *10 Story Western* (3/46), or his activities as a state legislator in "Derringers for Democracy" in *10 Story Western* (3/47). Defever, while no gunfighter, manages rather well with the Derringers he keeps concealed in his inside coat pockets.

Another series character was Juan Poker. These stories,

such as "Juan Poker's White Flag" in *10 Story Western* (4/45), are dependent even more than the Defever tales on a continuous string of action episodes with only the sketchiest setting and no elaborate characterization. In "Juan Poker—Registrar of Death" in *10 Story Western* (7/45) Blackburn sketched in Poker's background more fully than he had previously, and described his mission as a "one-man battle for justice and peace among the mixed peoples who farmed and mined and built cities on the edge of the Pacific."

Some of the fiction Blackburn wrote for *Dime Western*, while not using any series characters, retained this characteristic emphasis on action at the expense of characterization. "Call for Prairie Outcasts" in *Dime Western* (11/44) is about a wagon master who deserts overland freighting to command a river scow with 100 tons of freight beset by gunfights and a pitched battle on the river's shore. "Wanted—Single-Jack Fighting Men" in *Dime Western* (1/45) is in many ways a reprise of "Boomer King of the Footlight Trail" with its rivalry between two mining companies seeking to dominate the mines in the district. Yet, more typically, as in "Give Us a Sucker to Hang!" in *Dime Western* (6/48) with its plot of an innocent man confronted by a lynch mob and having to demonstrate in these desperate circumstances who the actual culprit is—one of the lynchers—Blackburn abandoned action to focus on a compact, concisely plotted suspense story. When two Blackburn stories were run in the same issue of *10 Story Western*, Tom used Steve Herrington as a pseudonym for the second story (utilizing his mother's maiden name), whereas in the other Popular Publications Western pulps he was assigned one of the house names, usually Ray P. Shotwell or Dave Sands.

It was for Fiction House that Blackburn wrote some of

his best stories in the middle 1940s. They are invariably of novelette length with sufficient space for him to develop both character and such themes as that of the two heroines— which Haycox had originally borrowed from Sir Walter Scott and used frequently in his magazine serials. The backgrounds are always intriguing. While sufficient latitude must be granted for the Fiction House tendency toward garish titles, in "Renegade Lady of the Blazing Buckhorn" in *Lariat Story Magazine* (1/44) Russ Cameron is an agent who buys up ranches for a Chicago speculator for resale. Sue McKenzie, the Taprock telegrapher, and Rae Orr, owner of the Chain Ranch, are the two heroines and they actually come to dominate the story. Occasionally a mystery element might be added as in the case of independent claims investigator Steve Archer in "Bullets Sang in Siesta" in *Lariat Story Magazine* (11/44) who is retained by the Great Republic Insurance Company to verify that the death of Jonas McClintock who owned a huge ranch near Siesta was an accident. The plot is further complicated by a woman who impersonates McClintock's only heir. Her background is filled in no less than that of the actual niece's. In "Trigger-Boss of Wild Horse Creek" in *Lariat Story Magazine* (5/45) environmental themes are joined with the theme of the two heroines. Ceasar Pendrake has convinced the ranchers in the district to invest in his scheme to irrigate the flatlands by constructing a dam. "This valley was peerless graze. It would never be anything else. Sod held the topsoil against wind and rain. Tilled crops could never do it. Irrigation would make a desert in time where grass now grew." In addition to a riveting plot, "Hostage of the Man-Pack" in *North-West Romances* (Spring, 50) generates a haunting image when its confrontation scene occurs in a sacred cavern on an Aleutian island where the bodies of Aleuts stretching back centuries and mummified by the intense cold seem to be ghostly apparitions surrounding the principal characters.

"Epitaph for a Boomtown Marshal" in *Zane Grey's Western Magazine* (7/49) was rightfully selected as a Zane Grey Award story and reprinted in the collection *Zane Grey Western Award Stories* (Dell Books, 1951). It is a tale dependent almost entirely on character for its tension, as was the case with many of Blackburn's earliest stories. Jack Dall is a town marshal who has in the opinion of the merchants outlived his usefulness, but Dall knows that trouble is brewing from the saloon owners' faction. Bob Francher originally got Dall the position and Dall ended up marrying Francher's girl, Marian. In the showdown Bob sides Dall who, except for his wife's support, is now alone. Dall's final thoughts as he is expiring have to do with what has been most important in his life: "He was leaving Bob Francher something wonderful, but there was a part of it Bob would never have. Her first love, just as it had been in the beginning. He knew Francher would not begrudge him this. He was losing so much else. . . . A man did his job as he saw it. Beyond this and beyond love, there was nothing."

Beginning in 1947 there was a new sense of depth to Blackburn's magazine fiction, as reflected in this story and others he wrote in those years. To handle his more traditional efforts he hired Frank P. Castle to work as his secretary, transcribing stories he would dictate, polish, proof, and send them off to Blackburn's agent, August Lenniger. Castle learned the trade well from this experience, as had Blackburn from his association with Repp, and by 1950 Frank Castle was publishing Western fiction under his own name. However, the most significant events that happened to Blackburn in the late 1940s were that he wrote and published his first novel and began his long-time association with the motion picture industry as a screenwriter.

Short Grass (Simon and Schuster, 1947) was dedicated to Juanita. It is perhaps worth noting that the preponderance of Blackburn's principal female characters in his novels are of Spanish-American or Mexican-American origin. That, however, was not the case with Juanita's ethnic heritage and it is not the case with the principal female character in this novel. The plot is also far more complex and sweeping than any of the short fiction Blackburn was writing at the time for magazines, although this novel was an expansion of a story Blackburn had titled "Man from the Short-Grass" that had earlier appeared under the title "The Gun-Prophet of Helldorado" in *Action Stories* (2/43). Steve Lewellyn is a drifter who happens by accident into the middle of a robbery and finds himself subsequently wounded from a bullet, fired by one of the bandits who he kills, and in possession of the loot. When Steve rides up to the Lynch Ranch, he discovers Sharon Lynch who is bathing in the nude. He falls from his horse unconscious as a result of his injury. Pete Lynch, Sharon's father, is an old man. Pete wants the additional range in Long Draw that is also coveted by Hal Fenton and his brother Randee. It was Fenton who had sent the men to rob the safe in La Mesa because he needed the money to buy Long Draw. Pete, suspecting that Steve has the loot, proposes to take him in as a partner if he'll invest the money in purchasing the coveted Long Draw. What complicates this narrative is not the events in the plot but rather the motives and beliefs of the characters. Steve soon realizes that Sharon hates the *llanos* and "that there was nothing Pete could build on the *llanos* which Sharon would want when her father was gone." Sharon does not believe in violence and opposing the Fentons will lead to violence.

She closes her ears to Steve's argument that a " 'man wasn't made to walk backwards' " and that, when challenged by the ruthless expansionism of a Fenton, a man has no choice but to fight to prevent it. " 'Backing up is a thing that gets to be a habit,' " he tells her, and he believes that "no man could make a truce with trouble." Although Sharon and Steve make love one night when they are alone at the ranch, after Steve goes over to the Fenton place and has a run-in with Randee Fenton that ends with Fenton dead, Sharon rejects Steve and wants nothing more to do with him. Steve leaves the *llanos* and homesteads outside Brokenbow, Kansas. Not only is the maturity of this plot a characteristic Blackburn shared with Les Savage, Jr., but also, as Savage, Blackburn ventured beyond the prototypical plot devised by Ernest Haycox that was so widely imitated at the time.

There is the theme of the two heroines but it has been transmuted. Zoe Barnage, daughter of the couple that owns the hardware store in Brokenbow, sets her hat for Steve, but he resists his attraction to her. "She would bend his back to a plow, his thinking to the security of their own possessions. And she would take him to bed. It wasn't enough." Sharon arrives in town, married to John Devore, a newspaperman and printer who opens up his business there. The marriage is not a happy one and Sharon finds herself taking Ord Keown, a noted gunfighter who is the town marshal, as her lover. It is Zoe's mother, Ruth Barnage, who is most sympathetic to Sharon's plight. " 'That's what makes marrying different than breeding cows,' " she tells Steve. " 'Mismatching don't bring good. I'm sorry for Sharon Devore. . . .' " Significantly absent is that stereotypical Western dichotomy of female characters into chaste angels and promiscuous whores that some writers such as Richard S. Wheeler would continue even into the 1990s. When Devore confronts Keown with a gun and is shot to death by the marshal, Steve covers for both Keown and Sharon by calling it a suicide, which, in a sense, is true. There is a dramatic confrontation between the town's citizens and Fenton who now, as a great rancher (he bought out Pete Lynch on *his* terms before Pete died), brings his rowdy drovers to town on a regular basis to ship beef to the East. In a humorous scene, reminiscent of Bret Harte, one of the townsmen, Kei Lin, is present at a meeting of fellow merchants at the Barnage home. Jed Barnage tells him to close the door to the parlor after Marshal Keown leaves. "The Chinese crossed the room. In the doorway Kei Lin made some gesture and spat almost silently into the outer hall." When Fenton is downed in the shoot-out at the end, it is Kei Lin—and not Steve—who pulls the trigger. When Steve and Sharon are at last united, it is as changed human beings, both wiser for the mistakes they have made and stronger for them. Sharon wants to return to the *llanos* and " 'the grass and our own brand and the heat and the dust and the room to be right and sure . . . always.' "

Raton Pass was featured in a condensed version as "Hired Guns and Badlands Beef" in *Zane Grey's Western Magazine* (11/50). Blackburn dedicated the novel to Howard and Edith and his godparents, Antime and Ethol. The narrative structure is not so strung-out as that of *Short Grass* with the time lapse here at the very beginning. The first scene shows Marcy Bennett "nursing" Ed Bennett along in order to speed his death and get access to his money because she has designs to marry Marc Challon and intends to be in Trinidad, New Mexico by winter. Following this prologue, the first chapter finds Marc and his father Pierre Challon in the living room of the great XO Ranch confronted by Marcy who wants a divorce so she can marry Anson Prentice, scion of a railroad magnet. Marc owes Anse $60,000 he borrowed to put in a dam on the Torrentado. For $130,000 more he agrees to sell out his remaining share of XO and then the two of them will have everything. The only thing Marc plans to take are 100 head of breeding stock.

Hank Bayard, the XO foreman, and the rest of the XO crew stay on with Marc. Marcy hires Cy Van Cleave, a hardcase killer from Lincoln County with his gang of cutthroats, to replace the crew. Although there are action episodes, what creates the real tension in this novel is the conflict of emotions and the cross-purposes of the characters. Fully sixteen years before Luke Short's *Paper Sheriff* (Bantam, 1966), Blackburn has his protagonist married to an unscrupulous woman. In only a vague sense is there a variation on the theme of the two heroines insofar as Marc enlists the help of Elena Casamajor. 'Lena has always been in love with Marc but he has some maturing to do before he discovers that he also loves her. Once he knows it, he recognizes that, in contrast to the carnality of his relationship with Marcy, 'Lena is "in his blood; she was the fiber of his being." Marc tells Anse that, unlike Marcy, Belle Challon may have come from a brothel in Kansas City, but she " 'was honest. She married an old man and gave him life and a home and happiness. She gave him faith. She gave him a son. She was my mother.' " Blackburn was also at equal pains to upset another stereotype to be found even in Harvey Fergusson's New Mexican fiction: "The legend of wantonness in Spanish-American women was not something that had grown on the grass itself, but among those who came onto it as outlanders. And beyond the exceptions which proved the rule, it was wholly untrue." Marc eventually regains the XO but only after much hardship and pain and what proves a terrible psychological ordeal to all of the principal characters and which, in various ways, costs Pierre, Marcy, and Anse their lives. The narrative does not end with a dramatic shoot-out, as does *Short Grass*, but with Marc handcuffing Van Cleave for his depredations. "Afterward," the reader is told, there were "Challons forever on the grass of New Mexico as well as under it—Challons with the sun-dark skins of the clean blood of the land."

Navajo Canyon (Doubleday, 1952) was serialized in four parts in *Ranch Romances* during January and February, 1952. It has greater unity of time and place than Blackburn's previous novels and narrates circumstances, both fictional and historical, concerned with Kit Carson's rounding up of the Navajo nation at the Cañon de Chelly and transporting it to the Bosque Redondo. Rick Lindquist, an Army scout, is the protagonist and, breaking tradition as Peter Dawson and T.T. Flynn had before him, he is a man no longer young. As Lindquist has discovered "suddenly one morning there is frost in the beard and in the hair when there is none on the ground. Blankets are warmer than they should be an hour after sunup. Old hurts are stiff. So swiftly as this, youth is gone. It is not old age, for this comes slowly. But a divide has been passed. The trail leads on as always, but it climbs no more peaks. The steady time is at hand. To some it is welcome." In a clever use of Frank Bonham's reversal on the theme of the two heroines, Lindquist and Lieutenant Steve Grayson are both romantically interested in Micaela Castaneda, the daughter of a Spanish *don* who has grown up in the Cañon de Chelly as a friend of the Navajos. Blackburn accomplished a considerable feat in that he generates sympathy for the Navajos' right to their traditional camping grounds *and* for Carson who is charged with removing them. Blackburn also observes that the friction between Indians and settlers is due mostly to a "mutual wariness . . . [that] seemed a more believable explanation for the increasing conflict along the frontier than any basis of cupidity among the whites or savagery among the Indians."

While he was still working as a magazine writer, Blackburn was hired to write a screenplay based on his magazine story of the same title which became upon release *Killer at Large* (Eagle Lion, 1947), a melodrama starring Robert Lowery and Anabel Shaw. Then in 1949 he was hired to work in the story department at Warner Bros. The first script he was given was an existing property titled *Colt .45* and "a boy from the story department wheeled in a hand truck similar to that used in grain stores to truck sacks of feed grain out to the loading dock and there was on that stack on the hand truck perhaps twenty-five or thirty separate scripts each by a different writer, each titled *Colt .45*, and each in various stages of finish—a few pages, or many, depending on the previous chap's luck. I took a look at the stack and refused to read any of them and started out from scratch and, lo and behold, they made my script. And this was not an unusual happening." It proved a fine action vehicle for Randolph Scott, but no more. However, it did subsequently form the basis for the successful television series "Colt .45" (ABC, 1957-1961) that starred Wayde Preston. Blackburn also moved into radio where he scripted thirteen episodes of "Tales of the Texas Rangers" (NBC, 1951) that featured Joel McCrea, and he was not above working on a "B" Western with Daniel Ullman like *Cavalry Scout* (Monogram, 1951). He was also able to script screen versions of his first two novels, *Short Grass* (Allied Artists, 1950) and *Raton Pass* (Warner, 1951).

Jack L. Warner was in the process of breaking what

Foreword

studio contracts he could because of the financial threat of television. He hired Blackburn to work on a film titled *Cattle Town* (Warner, 1952). He wanted to break Dennis Morgan's contract or at least place him on suspension (during which time he would not be paid) for refusing to do the picture. Warner wanted Blackburn to write a screenplay Morgan hated and one in which a great deal of stock footage lifted from previous films was to be interpolated. "To make things more certain," Blackburn later recalled, "Mr. Warner hired Brian Foy . . . to be his producer because he wanted to break Brian's contract, too, and next he hired a gentleman named Noel Smith, an old-time silent picture director, and he had the library probably research all the stock Western songs for Dennis to record instead of writing new music for the show which was the usual practice at the time. Not only did Dennis have old songs to sing but he also recorded them on location with unshielded microphones so that his really quite good voice was enhanced with wind sound going by the microphone. As a further device Mr. Warner looked about for an ingénue to play the female lead and finally found a cute little girl from Puerto Rico . . . and she turned out to be Rita Moreno. The upshot of it all was Dennis Morgan read my script and loved it; he liked his leading lady; he liked his producer. As a matter of fact, his comment to me was: 'Hell, Tom . . . I'd dig outhouses for one hundred and fifty thousand a picture.' " Even Jack L. Warner came out. The film made money.

Motion picture money and, later, television work permitted Blackburn to pursue a lifestyle that was widely envied by his fellow Western writers. When his agent, August Lenniger, would come to Los Angeles to visit, he would stay at Blackburn's home in Burbank. Lenniger invited clients D.B. Newton and Walker Tompkins to come down

from Santa Barbara, where they lived, and to have lunch at
Blackburn's home. "Two-Gun" Tompkins's response was:
"That would be rubbing my nose in it." After all, while the
nabobs of Santa Barbara had their polo ponies' names
stenciled on the doors of their Cadillacs, "Two-Gun" had a
jalopy that sported the sign: **Canta Forda Rancho**. They
lunched at the Beverly Wilshire instead. Subsequently, at
an informal meeting of the Fictioneers at Les Savage's
home in Santa Monica, William Campbell Gault, talking
confidentially in the kitchen to others in the group, complained how Blackburn who was a member of their group
(although obviously not present on this occasion) was letting success swell his head. "It was in this very kitchen,"
Gault said, "that I heard Tom sounding off about how he
expected some of his stuff would live. Hell! Somerset
Maugham's not going to live! How can you talk to a guy
like that?"

In the mid 1950s Blackburn worked in the story department at Walt Disney's studio and it was there, in addition
to working on the Davy Crockett films and teleplays
(among other projects), that he also began composing
lyrics. Among his most successful efforts are "The Ballad of
Davy Crockett" and "Farewell" for that series and "Johnny
Tremain" and "The Liberty Tree" for *Johnny Tremain*
(Buena Vista, 1957). It is not surprising that during this
same decade Blackburn's published Western fiction should
have been considerably reduced. He wrote *Sierra Baron*
(Random House, 1955), a novel employing the familiar
theme of a powerful rancher much in the Marc Challon
mode, which Blackburn also sold for the screen. He contributed a rather fragmented novelette titled "Buckskin
Man" to the anthology *Riders West* (Dell Books, 1956), but
he redeemed the story subsequently by expanding it artfully

and gracefully in the far more satisfying *Buckskin Man* (Dell Books, 1958).

It wasn't until *A Good Day To Die* (McKay, 1967), dedicated to his daughter Stephanie, that Blackburn returned to the Western novel. It was the most historically researched of any fiction he had yet written and it may well stand as his masterpiece. Set in the twilight years of the great Sioux nation, it narrates in gripping and powerful imagery and unforgettable characters the starvation of the People—as the Sioux called themselves—and the sudden, ultimately tragic appearance of an Indian Messiah who brings with him the "ghost dance" that cannot restore the buffalo, as he believes it will, but that instead leads to the massacre at Wounded Knee. Against this dramatic background is played out the love story between Chance Easterbrook, a correspondent for the New York *Herald*, and Shining Woman, daughter of a Sioux chief, and the doomed love Beau Lane feels for a white schoolteacher while drawn in the opposite direction by his blood heritage.

With *Yanqui* (Dell Books, 1973) Blackburn published the first volume in his Stanton saga that, in its five volumes, would chart the beginnings and growth of Spencer Stanton's land empire in New Mexico. Banished forever is the image of the strong man who can stand alone. Blackburn had come to believe that no one accomplishes anything by himself. Entering New Mexico when it was still under Mexican rule, Stanton forms deep and abiding friendships with Jaime, a young runaway from the East and an indentured servant, with Chato among the Utes, with Sol Wetzel, a Jewish merchant in Santa Fé, and above all with 'Mana—who turns out to be more Spanish than Ute, for it is she who brings with her the title to that land that will henceforth bear Stanton's Corona brand. In 'Mana it was as if all the heroines who had for so long embodied Juanita's sterling qualities at last found their ultimate expression in this bewitching, strong, inspiring woman. It is small wonder at the conclusion of the first volume that "for the first time in his life, Spencer Stanton, a hard and disillusioned man with many other weaknesses, wept. He had found his strength." *Ranchero* (Dell Books, 1974) is concerned with Stanton's defense of Corona; *El Segundo* (Dell Books, 1974) with telling Jaime Henry's story; and *Patrón* (Dell Books, 1976) and *Compañeros* (Dell, 1978) with the generation of Spencer's and 'Mana's son Tito. The Stanton saga is likely to stand as one of the major achievements in Western fiction. It also marked the end of Blackburn's professional career as an author. Juanita had fallen ill.

Having moved from Burbank to Newport where Blackburn owned a sailboat, Tom devotedly stayed by Juanita's side until her death in 1984. Increasingly lonely with Juanita gone, Tom was invited by his daughter Stephanie to come to Colorado to live with her. They lived together in Denver for three years before moving to Redstone where Blackburn spent the last years of his life, complicated by a series of strokes, in a beautiful valley surrounded by the mountains he had always loved. He died on August 2, 1992 in Glenwood Springs, Colorado. A blue spruce tree was planted in his memory in the park in Redstone.

In an extraordinarily successful career that spanned nearly four decades, Tom W. Blackburn contributed to the Western story in just about every format, from pulp and slick magazine fiction, novels, motion picture screenplays and adaptations, to radio dramas and teleplays. He even wrote lyrics to translate the Western experience into song. Based on such early novels as *Short Grass* as well as the later, far greater artistry to be found in *A Good Day to Die* and the Stanton saga, perhaps (if he ever said it) Blackburn's claim in Les Savage's kitchen was more true than false, for his legacy is one that is not very likely to date. His best fiction is concerned with the struggles, torments, joys, and the rare warmth that comes with companionships of the soul, the very stuff which is as imperishable in its human significance as the "sun-dark skins of the clean blood of the land" that he celebrated and transfixed in shimmering images and unforgettable characters.

River Raiders

Tom W. Blackburn sent this story titled "River Raiders" to his agent, August Lenniger, on October 18, 1947. It was sent on to Mike Tilden at Popular Publications, who purchased it for *Star Western* on November 3, 1947. The author was paid $195 at 2½¢ a word. Tilden, who usually changed the title of every story in an issue according to an agenda he had devised to pique a reader's interest when scanning the Table of Contents page, altered the title of the story to "Big Muddy Hell-Ship!" for its appearance in *Star Western* (3/48). It was the first of the five Cole Lavery stories, a series that would prove difficult for a reader to follow since subsequent stories would appear in a variety of Popular Publications magazines.

I

The river was huge, silent, oily, yellow with silt, even in the moonlight. The *Missouri Pride* bucked the current, shivering with the slow vibration of the huge paddle wheel churning astern. Captain Farrell was leaning against the foredeck railing at Cole Lavery's elbow. The captain had been drinking a little since dinner. And he smelled always of poor eating tobacco. Lavery wished Farrell would go away. The girl was on deck, too, clearly visible in the forepeak, and Lavery had been waiting two days for a chance to talk with her, alone. But the whiskey apparently felt good in Farrell's belly. He wanted to talk.

"Westbound," he said. It was a statement rather than a question. "Who isn't? The whole damned country on the move. To California. Gold. And the ones coming back with empty pockets don't stop them heading West. They got to go. You, too, eh? You're headed for California?"

Lavery looked at the girl in the forepeak, a slender figure standing against the night wind that pressed the looseness of her traveling dress close about her.

"I don't know," Lavery said, thinking he might possibly go where this girl went. He didn't really know. Captain Farrell eyed him sharply, studying the clean cut of his figure, the steadiness of his features, the quietness of his voice.

Farrell shook his head. "I reckon you don't," he agreed. "Only old men know where they're going. By God, if I was young again. . . ." He broke off. Lavery thought he was looking at the girl, for a moment, then he saw the riverman was only looking up the yellow river. "But I ain't young," Farrell went on after a moment. "And I've got my job. This damned little packet ain't much, but she's got a big job. She's got to haul thousands of people to the beginning of the grass . . . whole towns of them. She's got wagon parts and hardware and machinery and arms and grubstakes to haul in. She's got money to haul in, so folks can trade."

He paused again. Lavery gave him no encouragement. It was getting a little cooler. The girl might leave. The captain looked again at Lavery, his eyes this time resting on the gun belt with its scarred holster, its powder flask and leather shot pouch and brass cap case.

"You can use that?" he asked suddenly.

Lavery glanced at his holstered weapon. "I started in Iowa and I've got this far," he said dryly.

"All right," the captain of the *Missouri Pride* said. "You're going to need what stake you can hang onto and I can't afford to hire a regular guard to ride the river with me. I've got thirty thousand dollars in minted gold coins in my cabin and there's one or two or maybe more boys on board that want it kind of bad. If they don't get it, I'll refund half your passage when we get to Westport Landing."

"You could be hiring one of the boys that wanted that gold," Lavery suggested.

"I could be, but I ain't," Farrell said positively. "That kind of boy wouldn't stand out here in the dark, waiting for the moon to get just right on the river afore he walked up to that girl. He'd bust right over the minute he seen her, if that was what he wanted. He wouldn't give a damn about the moon. His kind don't. And they're always headed some place specific. Afraid somebody'll suspect them if they don't."

"Who's after your gold?"

"It ain't my gold," Farrell answered. "Goes to a bank out at Westport. Maybe for Army payroll. Maybe for buying wagons or grub. Belongs to boys like you, fixing out there to head across the grass. And I aim to see it gets to them. Drift back into the smoking room directly. You'll find a gent back there that claims to be a Senator. He ain't. He's too smooth, too smart. Senators in this man's country are working men, son. And this one never done an honest day of sweat in his life. If there's trouble, it'll start with him."

The captain grinned friendliness, turned, and took the port catwalk around the main cabin, headed aft. Cole Lavery thoughtfully shifted the belt at his hips. He needed a little cash. Refund of half his passage money was worthwhile. And he found himself thinking about what Captain Farrell had said concerning the $30,000 in gold in his cabin. He found himself thinking that it was important that this money reached the Westport bank. It was important that the men on the edge of the grass had gold to work with. It was hard to buy things with empty pockets. Lavery knew this only too well. He found himself wanting to do something about getting that gold safely to the end of the run and he was dryly amused with himself. It wasn't his gold, and it wasn't his affair, and he was the man who had pulled out of the corn country with a determination to mind only his own business and his own desires.

Farrell had suggested he wait a little before going in to find the man who claimed to be a Senator. The girl was still at the forepeak. Lavery crossed to her with an easy, rolling stride, and removed his hat.

"Lavery is the name, ma'am," he said quietly. "Excuse me, but it's getting a little cold out here. . . ."

The girl turned. She was smaller than he had thought, and much prettier. An oval, tanned face, unpowdered, shining a little with freshness and health in the moonlight. Large eyes, widely spaced. Her straight nose was snubbed a little at the end. And full, very red, generous lips. There was a little fire in the eyes, and blandness, too, so that Lavery knew there was no pretense in her and no toleration of pretense in others. A stubborn girl, perhaps. Perhaps a difficult one. But of the kind about which men dream on remote nights when there is musk on the wind and the moon is warm.

"Cold?" she said.

"The wind," Lavery explained. "It's coming from the mountains."

The girl smiled a little. "I'm quite comfortable, thank you," she answered. "There's a lot of sun between here and the mountains, Mister Lavery. The wind seems quite warm."

"Not many people know how far the mountains are from the Missouri," Lavery said. "You're going that far?"

"Maybe," the girl said. "I don't know."

So she didn't know how far she was going, either. Lavery smiled. He tried to think of something else to say. He could not reach out his hands and lay them on a strange girl, no matter how much he wanted to. There were things to be said, first.

"Look," the girl said suddenly. "My name is Marta Strand. I have a trunk full of clothes. I sing, if I have a chance, or I dance. I don't know where I'm going. I like the moonlight. Maybe I like your face. No, I don't talk with strange men, but you've tried to be nice. I'll try, too. I'll talk with you. But not now. Later. After I've sung in the smoker."

Lavery grinned crookedly. He had been right. She was direct. Very direct. And she drew a direct answer from him. "Sure, that's what I want. I didn't quite know how to say it. My first name is Cole. Cole Lavery. I move . . . from one place to another, looking. I'm sort of a guard, now, for part of my passage on this packet. I'm headed West, that's all. I'll hear you sing . . . then we'll talk. . . ."

"I'll come back here," Marta Strand said. She turned away, then looked back over her shoulder at Lavery. "What needs guarding on this packet?" she asked.

"Ask Captain Farrell," Lavery said.

The girl smiled and went down along the starboard rail. She knocked on the door of the smoking room and called out a name. The door opened almost immediately. Lavery had a glimpse of a small beard, a carefully kept mane of white hair, and a perfectly fitted coat. The girl stepped through the door and it closed.

II

Cole did not knock on the smoker door, but opened it unhurriedly and stepped into the room. Riverboat etiquette, limited as it was, did not permit the poisoning of the main cabin with either smoke or whiskey. As a consequence the bar was in the smoker, a comfortable square cabin, furnished, in addition, with settees and two game tables. Most of the male passengers on the packet were jammed into the room. It smelled of men and body heat and whiskey and Virginia leaf. It smelled restless. Two men were dragging a small, incredibly battered square case piano into position in one corner. Marta Strand was supervising their efforts.

Cole located the man who had met her at the door—unquestionably the same man who Farrell suspected had designs on the gold consignment his packet carried. Above his light beard his face was florid, but this deep coloring was not accompanied by the easy, good-natured eyes such men usually possessed. This man's eyes were faded, almost colorless, and had a peculiar fixed, frigid steadiness. Cole thought Farrell was right. The man was not a Senator. If he was, he was wasting his talents.

A number of others were gathered around the self-styled Senator, who was lounging easily in a big chair, his eyes running over a newspaper folded carefully in his lap. His eyes reached up to touch Cole for a moment as he came in the doorway, then dropped to the paper. He went on speaking to those grouped about him.

"So you think we're three years late, moving West? Rubbish! We're early, if anything. The movement is just beginning. Here we are, riding the rivers, with a long wagon trail ahead when we land. But here's an item. Donald McKay's shipyard in Boston has launched the *Flying Cloud*. Last year it was the *Staghound*. Next one, already started, is the *Sovereign of the Seas*. California Clippers. The way everybody will travel in another year. It's just the beginning. Here's a report on that Swedish singer Phineas Barnum brought over here, Jenny Lind. Singing in New Orleans now. Next year it'll be in Fort Laramie or Bridger City or maybe San Francisco. They'll grow, all of them."

"The California claims are all taken up, they say," a man ventured.

The Senator nodded curtly. "Of course. But gravel claims are for men who want to sweat." He paused, smiling suddenly. "Personally I don't like calluses on my hands. My boys keep their nails clean."

A man beside Cole turned to him and spoke under his breath. "What you think of the Senator?"

"I don't know," Cole answered. "What's he want?"

The Senator's hearing was acute. He sat a little forward. "I'll answer that, friend," he said to Cole. "I want a few honest, straightforward young men who are willing to take a little gamble. A few good boys with hell in their hearts. A hard-riding, hard-drinking bunch with a little hair on their chests who want something more out of life than four log walls and a sod roof. Boys with an ear for opportunity. Interested?"

"Maybe," Cole said.

The self-styled Senator nodded agreeably. "Think it over," he said. The men had finished moving the piano. Marta Strand was seated on the stool before it. The Senator

38

saw she was ready. He rose to his feet. "Gentlemen, as a gesture of good will, I have secured you a treat in entertainment. Miss Marta Strand, in songs a man would go a long way to hear."

The Senator sat down. Marta Strand began to play. Cole saw immediately she was nervous and in a moment more he realized that she did not know the kind of songs the Senator had promised. Men in a riverboat smoker on the Missouri did not want the sentimental old ballads they had left behind them. They wanted the acrid, smoky, sulphurous songs of the frontier, of women as big as the plains and as lusty. Even Cole himself did not want the old songs. He moved quietly to the door and let himself out on deck. He made himself a cigarette, lighted it, and leaned against the rail to watch the river sliding past. In a moment the door opened and closed again. A man moved to the rail beside him.

"Lavery is the name, isn't it?" the self-styled Senator asked. Cole nodded wordlessly. "Better be smart, Lavery," the man said. "Be as smart as you look. Somebody is going to make thirty thousand dollars."

"Somebody is going to be taken overboard on a plank if he tries," Cole said.

The Senator chuckled. "Sand," he said. "I like sand. Ever hear of Spade Garrison, Lavery?"

Cole had. The Garrison gang had made dangerous things of the Tennessee wilderness roads. It had once practically cut Kentucky off from the seaboard. It had become legend. A lot of Garrisons had been hanged. The gang had been broken up. But one Garrison had slipped through the net that caught the others. The most dangerous Garrison of them all. Cole nodded.

"Got that nickname because somebody thought my face

looked like a shovel," Spade Garrison said. "That was quite a while ago. Now who do you think might go overboard on a plank?"

"Depends on luck . . . and how many of those fools join up with you," Cole answered.

"Hell, I don't want any of them," Garrison said shortly. "I'm going to build up a bunch of boys here on the edge of the grass, but I'm not going about it that way. I want boys who are really good. I'll be having a meeting down in my cabin after a while. Most of those inside that could cause trouble will be there. And the girl inside will have moved into the main cabin to sing to the rest of the passengers. If this damned tub is on schedule, she'll be running along Cottonwood Flats then. There are horses waiting at the flats, Lavery."

"So you go over the side with better than a hundred pounds of metal. It won't float, Garrison."

"It goes over in a mail sack with a long rope tied to it. Ashore, it can be dragged in. There's thirty thousand dollars, Lavery. Twenty are mine. You could use the rest."

"What about the girl," Cole asked. "She in this?"

"If you want her. What she gets comes out of your cut. But she goes, if you want her. There are three horses waiting."

"I could say no," Lavery said, and shrugged his shoulders.

"Maybe you will," Garrison agreed. "It won't make any difference. And since you've asked about her, the girl will go, anyway. With me, if not with you. Emil Stone's in there, listening to her sing. I couldn't handle him long, but he'd do for tonight. He'd take care of the captain while I was having my little meeting in my cabin. He could take care of the girl. And I could take care of him tomorrow. Even before tomorrow."

"Stone is a good man with his gun. I've heard of him."

Garrison smiled. "I used to be fairly good myself, Lavery."

Cole swung slowly toward the man. "Why deal me in? Why not Stone, from the first?" he asked.

"I told you I wanted to build a bunch. Maybe I like your looks. Maybe it's only I know Farrell has made you an offer and I want to damn' well keep you off my neck tonight."

Cole shook his head. Spade Garrison shrugged.

"It's too bad, Lavery," he said. He sounded honestly regretful. "You don't give me any choice. I'm going to have to kill you sometime between now and midnight."

Cole nodded. "I reckon you'll have to try," he agreed.

Garrison looked at him a moment longer, then turned and walked easily away across the deck. Cole snapped his cigarette out over the water and turned as a scattering of half-hearted applause sounded in the smoker at his back. A moment later the door opened and Marta Strand came out. She walked swiftly past Cole toward the forepeak. In the light escaping the door Cole saw her face was clouded. He supposed she had learned something it would take her a little time to face—that however mean the motives, or however noble, for that matter, that turned a woman into a frontier entertainer, it took both skill and courage to face her audience. He didn't need to be told that this was the first time Marta had sung in a bar, possibly the first time in public. And now she understood that something she had thought would be easy had suddenly become difficult. He followed her forward at a slower pace.

III

Halfway up the line of cabins, a door opened. Cole halted, pivoted a quarter, and pressed his back against the deckhouse bulkhead. Spade Garrison came out. He glanced at Cole, smiled, shot his cuffs, and moved unhurriedly on back to the smoker door. Cole heard his voice rise in greeting to the men inside.

"A woman and a song . . . now the bottle. Belly up, boys. The Senator from Illinois is buying drinks."

Lavery pushed away from the bulkhead and moved on. As he came abreast Captain Farrell's cabin, he saw the door was open, the cabin dark. He paused, started toward the doorway.

"It's all right, Lavery," the riverman's voice came out of the darkness. "Was I right about the Senator?"

"Yes," Cole answered.

"When?" Farrell asked sharply.

"When you're off Cottonwood Flats. About midnight, I think."

"Midnight exactly," Farrell said. "I'll have the pilot watch his speed to put us there then, so you can figure time. Still interested in that half-fare refund?"

"If I'm still aboard," Cole agreed.

Farrell made a grunting, curious sound.

"The Senator is Spade Garrison," Cole went on. "He tried to buy me in with him. I turned him down."

"Garrison!" Farrell swore softly. "Look, son, we better go easy. Garrison's all no good. I'd rather lose the gold than have to unload half a dozen dead passengers. You get down in the fire room. That'll keep you off deck. Spade Garrison. Hell, let him have the money."

"I'm going to Westport, Captain," Cole said quietly.

"So's the gold. Might as well get there together. Besides, I don't like fire rooms and I need that refund. You climb back up to the pilot house. I'll watch your cabin."

"You're crazy, son," Farrell said.

"Sure," Cole agreed. "But there's tougher men than Spade Garrison out on the grass. I won't get far if I buckle to the first one I meet."

Farrell swore again. Cole moved on toward the forepeak. Behind him he heard the captain quit his cabin and climb swiftly toward the texas. Marta Strand was leaning on the bitt crowning the stem post.

Cole stopped quietly beside her. "Champagne will gag any gullet used to rotgut," he said.

"You know what they asked me to sing in there?" the girl asked.

Cole smiled a little. "I can guess," he said. "Want me to teach you the words?"

"They didn't even hear my voice. They didn't even know if I could sing. Just waiting for something ugly . . . some rotten song. They're rotten. All of them. Rotten!"

"Not all of them," Cole said. "Just some. Just a few. This is a big country, Miss Strand. Men grow big appetites. Their blood is closer to their skin. Those songs aren't as rotten as you think. They've just got a stronger flavor than you're used to. That's all. The whole frontier runs to stronger tastes."

"That's the kind of singing you like to hear, too?" she asked.

"It's who's singing that I listen to, not the song," Cole answered. "Learn what they want to hear. Sing it straight at them, honestly, so they know you're singing it for them, because they want it, not because it's what you want to sing. Do that and you'll get along, wherever you want to go."

The girl leaned back a little against Cole, looking up at him.

"I'm tired," she said.

"You're scared," Cole corrected. "It's all right. You'll get over it."

He bent and kissed her then. She stiffened for a moment, then eased. When he released her, she smiled a little, gratitude in her eyes for his gentleness.

"I've been lonely," she said.

"So have I," Cole told her. "We all are. Ten . . . twenty . . . fifty thousand people traveling the same trail, and every one of us lonely. Sometimes we're in too much of a hurry to make friends."

The girl's brows knit. "You mean?"

Cole laughed. "No, not us. The Senator from Illinois. When did you meet him?"

"At dinner tonight. Why?"

"Never saw him before?"

Marta Strand shook her head.

Cole spoke earnestly. "Somebody's going to ask you to sing again, in the main cabin this time. Do it. Keep singing till it's nearly midnight, say five minutes to. There's a clock in the bulkhead. You can watch it. When you're through, don't go back out on deck. Take the door with the little window in it. Leads back to the galley, I think. Go out that way. Go back there with the cook and stay till things are quiet."

"What's going to happen?" she asked sharply.

"Not much, I hope," Cole said. "But you've got to stay out of the way. The Senator figures on getting off the boat about midnight and he's got a notion he's going to take you with him."

"Me?" Marta paled. "Why?"

44

"Because he's got a notion I'll get reckless if he tries. You keep out of the way."

"Would you . . . get reckless, I mean?" Marta asked quietly.

"Yes," Cole told her evenly.

"I'll go into the kitchen, then," the girl said. Cole tightened his arm about her. Her face tilted up again. Their lips met. Footsteps sounded on the deck. A hostile perfume cut through the aura of the girl's fragrance. Cole looked up. A large, tired woman, one of the passengers, had approached.

"Excuse me, Miss Strand," the woman said uneasily. "My husband heard you sing in the smoker a few minutes ago. He thought we would all enjoy your songs. There's a piano in the main cabin. Would you mind?"

Marta looked at Cole. He nodded imperceptibly.

She turned to the woman. "No, not at all," she answered easily. "It's kind of you to ask."

Her fingers touched Cole's for a moment. Then she moved back down the deck with the other woman. Cole glanced up at the texas. He could see neither the pilot nor Captain Farrell. There were no lights in the pilot house. He looked at his watch. He had a half hour. Pushing out from the rail, he started aft. He had just passed the smoker door when it banged open. The unattached men passengers, those who might give trouble in case there was an alarm on the boat, followed Spade Garrison out, docile with his whiskey and the ring of his voice. He moved along the deck toward his cabin, speaking expansively to all of them.

"The Missouri Freighting Company. That's what we'll call our outfit, boys. And there's plenty of money for financing at Westport or Saint Joe. We won't put a dime of our own pocket money in. We'll offer the men and the brains. Let somebody else put up the coin, eh?"

There was mumbling, excited, incoherent assent. Cole swore softly. This was something he didn't understand. Men who in their own home country were sound and sensible citizens—men who had a grip on reality and knew well enough that a man didn't make a fortune out of nothing— were willing, even anxious, out here to believe any incredible proposition. And it seemed to him that the farther West he traveled, the more preposterous became the schemes in which they believed. Maybe it was something in the air, maybe it was that old horizons had suddenly expanded to embrace the whole almost unknown half of a continent. At any rate, Garrison had this bunch so wrapped up in speculation and whiskey that they wouldn't know it if the *Missouri Pride* hit a bar and broke her back.

One of the men who followed Garrison out turned in the opposite direction from the others and followed Cole toward the stern. Cole heard his footfalls along the planking of the deck. He didn't have to turn to know the man. Garrison was smooth. While the others were drinking, he'd had a few words with Emil Stone. A few words and a promise of a cut in $30,000 in gold. Now, while Garrison kept the men with him enthralled with prospects of a fortune to be made in a mythical freighting concern that would presently go over the packet's rail with Garrison—while the boss kept his hands clean, Stone was about to begin the dirty work.

IV

Stone was an opportunist, a Texan, Lavery had heard. A big man, hard as cap rock lava, with his whole nature turned bluntly outward for all to see. An arrogant, short-tempered, vain man with a legend of violence already at his

46

back and a hard, sure, unprincipled confidence. Cole was wholly aware of the ominous note in the man's footfalls. He thought he was afraid. There was a tightness in his belly and a sudden hot dryness in his mouth. He thought these things were fear.

He thought, also, that he was a damned fool, that he had been since the moment Captain Farrell had talked to him. He had been a fool with Garrison and with Marta Strand. Now he was about to play the fool with Stone. It didn't make sense. Garrison had offered him 100 times more than the niggardly refund that had been Farrell's bid. The risky side was with Farrell, too, not with Garrison. And he really didn't give a damn whether the gold in Farrell's cabin got to Westport or not. He wasn't even sure who it belonged to and he didn't care about that.

He had fumbled with Marta Strand, too. There was something about a boat moving on water. Something that cut it off from the rest of the world. Something that plowed under old restraints. Particularly in women. A man with a lonely girl in his arms on the forepeak of a packet in the moonlight didn't have to be gentle with his kisses—he didn't have to offer quiet advice. There weren't any rules that said he did. This was the frontier. If a man wanted a woman and she didn't run away, he took her.

Now, with Stone. . . . He was walking slowly down the deck with a notoriously fast gun handler at his back. He was walking slowly and unhurriedly, as though time was all on his side and the gun in the holster at his thigh as quick and lethal as any. It was damned foolishness, all of it. And there wasn't any better reason for the whole thing than the fact that Cole Lavery had been moving up the Missouri to start something where there was plenty of room for starting. Something he wasn't even sure of yet. Maybe land, maybe cattle, maybe fur, maybe freight. Maybe nothing. He knew only one thing for sure—when he began, he wanted to do it right.

Cole halted as he came up against the hood that separated the end of the port catwalk from the broad, slow-moving vanes on the great paddle wheel positioned across the stern of the *Missouri Pride*. The footfalls of the man behind came on. Cole turned unhurriedly, put the flat of his shoulder blades against the hood. Stone stopped two yards away in the darkness. A long, top-heavy figure, slouching a little on widely planted legs. Light glinted faintly from the white backs of his hands, usually gloved and now bare for the business at hand. Light also touched the gun gear at the man's belt and a brass or gold clasp that held the knot of the kerchief circling his neck under his collar.

Lavery had a momentary urge to tell Stone he was a fool, also. He wanted to tell Stone that maybe Garrison and himself would make it tonight, but that tomorrow, somewhere up on higher country back from the river, Spade Garrison would turn suddenly in his saddle. A gun would fire without warning. Emil Stone would die between one breath and the next. And Garrison would ride on with all of the gold that had been taken from this packet.

Instead, Cole drew tobacco and a paper from his pocket and carefully rolled a cigarette with his back pressed tightly against the paddle hood. When the smoke was between his teeth, he said: "Got a match, Stone?"

The man smiled slowly. Reaching into his pocket, he found a match and tossed it to Cole. As Lavery put the match against his nail to rasp it, Stone took an easy, rolling, backward step and his hand hooked in the air, a hand's breadth above his gun. Cole scratched the match, but with its first splutter, instead of raising it to his cigarette, he

snapped it with sharp suddenness straight at
As a part of the same movement, he thrust
against the hood at his back, flinging his body .

Stone dodged the little lance of fire that shot at
even in surprise the man was fast. As the match s
his dodging head, his gun slid clear of leather. Cole
in the center of the face as the weapon swept up.
reeled back another step and Cole caught the gun.
spinning motion that had the full drive of his legs
thighs behind it and his full weight for momentum,
caught Stone's gun and gun arm under one of his own arm,
pits and threw a twist on the arm. The gun clattered free,
unfired. Stone yelped, but was jerked forward on his toes
and driven, reeling, against the hood.

He rebounded dazedly from this and Lavery hit him
again. The man sagged. Cole scooped up the fallen gun
from the deck and made certain of the man's sagging with a
slicing chop of the barrel across Stone's ear. The man
grunted softly and fell loosely onto the planking. Cole
swung the gun and released it. It arched far out over the
river and fell with a small splash into the muddy current.
Turning, Cole walked rapidly back up the promenade past
the many cabin doors of the deckhouse.

The smoker door was open, swinging idly on its hinges
with the motion of the boat. The room was empty. Even the
galley crewman who doubled as steward and bartender was
gone from behind the bar. In the next compartment forward, which was the main cabin, Lavery heard the tinny ca-
dence of the piano, and an instant later Marta Strand's
voice followed. She had changed her songs, even for the
main cabin. They were quicker, lustier. And she had
changed her way of singing. Her voice had a strength and a
faster rhythm, like a quickened heartbeat. Cole smiled

iefly. She had understood what he had said.

Captain Farrell's cabin was still empty and dark. Cole eclosed the door. He eyed the ladder to the texas, wondering if he had time to climb up with a report to Farrell and a request that the riverman and the pilot stand by with their rifles. He decided against this. The time was important, and Garrison would have his plans laid well. He would be certain Farrell and the pilot and any stray crewmen stayed out of the whole thing. So sure, in fact, that they would likely never get into anything again. If Farrell and the pilot came out of the pilot house at the wrong time, they would be dead men. No use risking that.

Turning on toward the bow, Cole circled the forward end of the deckhouse and started back down the opposite promenade. He didn't know where Garrison's cabin was, but he found it easily. The lamps were bright in it. Tobacco smoke boiled out through the ventilator in the door. The muted sound of men's voices talking excitedly in a small room also came through the ventilator. And above this murmur, Garrison's voice rang occasionally, apparently selling the drunken and exuberant men with him a bill of goods and a quick way to riches, but actually only keeping them off of the deck and out of the way.

Lavery looked at his watch. He had ten minutes until midnight. In five minutes Marta Strand would quit singing in the main cabin. When she did, Garrison would have to move. If he didn't, the crowd gathered there would pour out onto the deck and in a few minutes he would have more witnesses to his business on board the *Missouri Pride* than he'd want.

Cole wanted to go aft again far enough to see Stone's body. He knew he had not hit the man hard enough. Stone's kind would not stay down long with that kind of a

belting. And when the man was back on his feet, personal injury would make him twice as savage as was his usual nature. Cole knew he should have killed Emil Stone at the paddle hood, while he had the chance. The justification had been there. But somehow it was very hard to kill a man when there was another way. He hoped Stone would stay unconscious for a few minutes longer—long enough to upset Garrison's plans. Long enough to make Garrison work out his business alone. Garrison, after all, could not wait for a better time. The pilot would take the packet past Cottonwood Flats at exactly midnight. If Garrison was to reach his horses, he had to go over then.

Swinging forward again, Cole crossed the ship and dropped back to Farrell's cabin. He let himself into this, shot the latch on the door, and sank back on the captain's bunk. Farrell occupied a standard passenger cabin. The interior features were like those of any other. Cole was grateful for this. Because of it, he was on familiar ground. He didn't need a light. There was the door and a porthole in the bulkhead. These were the only openings. Cole studied the room, then stretched himself out on the deck along the base of the outboard bulkhead with his feet under the porthole and his torso across the sill of the door itself.

In a moment another thought struck him. Rising, he hauled the mattress and bedding from the bunk, creased the mass length-wise through the middle, and stood it up in the diagonal corner. Poking the blanket in here and there to conceal the whiteness of the sheets Captain Farrell affected, he put his own hat on top of the clumsy, standing roll of bedding. Satisfied, he stretched out along the base of the outboard bulkhead again.

Somewhere astern something ceased and Cole had the feeling of a sudden silence, although the normal sounds of the ship continued without change. He thought he knew what it was. Marta Strand had reached the end of her song. It was five minutes until midnight. He needed now luck and patience. . . .

The interior of the captain's cabin was so dark Lavery could not see his watch after he had drawn it from his pocket. The steady, unhurried vibration of the *Missouri Pride*'s long-reaching compound engines was monotonous under him. There was no movement apparent on the deck, at least on this side of the packet. The piano in the main cabin had commenced tinkling again, but with a different style than when Marta Strand had accompanied herself and he thought someone else had sat down to take up where she had left off. He became convinced of this a moment later when the player made the amateur's inevitable error and a chord went sour.

Cole had it figured completely. Garrison would quit his cabin, excusing himself from those he was entertaining for a moment. Unsuspecting, they would remain where they were, waiting for him. He would make a quick circuit of the deck in search of Emil Stone. Maybe he'd find Stone up. Maybe the man would still be down. In any event, Garrison would learn his plans for Cole Lavery had gone a little astray. Working close on time with Cottonwood Flats already drifting past the rail, Garrison would have no choice. He would come directly to the captain's cabin, knowing the gold he wanted was there and probably fully aware that Cole would be waiting there for him, too. So Garrison would make his try and so would Cole Lavery. One or the other of them would come out on the lucky side. In any event, it would be over quickly. There wasn't much more of this crawling, unpleasant waiting. There wasn't much more guessing.

Cole did not feel the first heel of the packet. Or if he did, he thought it was merely a roll of the boat against a current in the river. But suddenly a sixth sense warned him that the *Missouri Pride* had shifted course. She was not running in the same direction she had been. She was not squarely bucking the current of the river. She was angling across it. Cole came to his feet, and, as he did so, the old packet shoved her nose into the mud of a riverbank with a gentle shock. She stopped moving, although her paddle wheel continued to churn with deliberate steadiness.

Cole tore open the door of the cabin. Brush was almost in his face. He could see the light of the fire, back on the grass. He could see the men running down. And suddenly he saw a great many other things he should have seen before, things that set him to swearing with a quiet fluency at his own stupidity. He was a prize damned fool!

Farrell had sung a sweet song, but Farrell was a blackleg. He didn't give a damn about the gold in his cabin. Likely as not, there wasn't any coin shipment consigned to a Westport bank. Maybe there wasn't even a bank at Westport. Captain Farrell and Spade Garrison were playing the same cards. And they were playing them together. A very smooth game. There were perhaps fifty men on the packet, all westbound. Not all of them were empty of pocket, like Cole Lavery. A lot of them would be carrying their stake with them, the means with which they intended to set themselves up again in a new country—Kansas or The Nations or the Rockies or Oregon or even California. The total take in their pockets was a good deal more than thirty thousand dollars. Garrison and Farrell wanted that.

Garrison had posed as a Senator. That might stick when the robbed passengers told their stories to the helpless authorities at the end of the run. It wouldn't matter if it didn't. Garrison would be carried away, howling protest, by the men racing through the timber toward the grounded ship. And Captain Farrell would be in the clear. Hadn't he hired Mr. Cole Lavery as guard, all in good faith? Would he deliberately run his precious packet into the mud? One of the hold-up gang must have gotten aboard. A masked man had put a gun into the pilot's back and forced him to run ashore. A hell of a note when a skipper who was willing to risk his boat on the snags and bars of the Big Muddy couldn't do his navigating in peace. While all this was going on, the man hired to guard the packet lay on the floor of the captain's cabin, waiting for someone to try stealing something that wasn't there.

Cole plunged onto the deck. Twenty feet away, two men were leaning over the rail, watching the men racing toward the grounded steamer. Past them, the door of the main cabin was open and a few of the women and married men within it had come out on deck, startled by the jar of the grounding. As Lavery hit the deck, the two men wheeled toward him. One was Emil Stone. The man swore. The other was Spade Garrison. Cole saw Garrison pass his companion a gun. Stone lunged toward him. Cole wheeled and raced around the forward end of the deckhouse. The door of Garrison's cabin had opened and some of those within had staggered into the outer air. Cole seized the first of these, a man who seemed somewhat sobered by the shock of grounding.

"Hold-up!" he said tersely. "Get a bunch into the engine room. Make the crew down there back their engines. They can do it. Make them get us off the mud. Pour the steam to her!"

The man nodded quick comprehension and seized a couple nearest to him. The three ran toward the door at the head of the fire room ladder. Cole doubled back forward and hooked the ladder rising on this side to the texas. He was half up this when Stone loped around the forward end of the deckhouse. Cole unhung his gun and slammed a quick shot at the man. Stone went flat, rolled, and ducked back around the deckhouse. Cole reached the texas, grabbed the pull rope on the whistle, and tied it down with a quick hitch around a projecting nail in the pilot house structure.

A woman screamed high above the deep roar of the whistle. A gun began to bang rhythmically. Cole was suddenly aware that he was visible from the forepeak and that Emil Stone had opened up on him from there. He ducked flat against the sidewall of the pilot house and dropped back toward the door. This flew open and Captain Farrell appeared in the opening, a heavy, short-barreled rifle across his hip. The piece fired once, the concussion at such close range jolting Cole, but the shot went a little wide.

"Drop it!" he snarled at Farrell. The man was slow. Cole fired his own gun. Farrell staggered, dropped the rifle, and commenced to bellow loudly with hurt, both hands digging into one thigh. Lavery shouldered him out of the way and slid on into the pilot house. The pilot, half drunk and very afraid at sight of the blood staining Farrell's trouser leg, was pressed back against his wheel. Cole seized him and swung him about to face it.

"Get us off of this mud now!" he charged. And at this instant, the big wheel astern stopped rotating, paused for a moment, and began to churn in a reverse direction. The pilot glanced in astonishment at the fire room telegraph, still set at **Half-Ahead.** Then he seized the spokes of his wheel.

Lavery ducked back out onto the texas. Emil Stone had

Tom W. Blackburn

dropped down beside a crate lashed up forward for steadiness. As Cole reappeared, he fired. A hard blow spilled Cole flat, dropping him under another slug that cut in from nearer at hand. He thought his leg had been torn off. He rolled almost to the rail of the hurricane deck under the sledging of pain from the wound. Spade Garrison's ugly, groomed face was at the top of the ladder, his gun leveling. Cole swung his own weapon. Garrison ducked down.

The men racing toward the packet from the fire ashore were almost to her rail. Her nose was still in the mud although her paddles were churning an increasingly spectacular froth astern and her whole hull was shuddering with effort. Lavery rose to his knees. He wasn't sure how many charges he had in his gun, but the odds were already steep enough on board. Those ashore must be kept from climbing the rail. His weapon fired three times. He thought he spilled one man. Then the weapon *clicked* futilely. Cole surged unsteadily to his feet, clinging to the rail, and flung the gun downward at Garrison, who still clung to the ladder, his head low.

The weapon struck Garrison on the shoulder sharply enough to jar him loose. He fell to the deck. One of the passengers now beginning to crowd the decks under the stentorian urgings of the whistle and the bang of gunfire stared upward at Cole.

"Hey, what is this?"

Garrison got his feet under him, rocked back and, from his haunches, snapped a shot upward. It brushed Cole, pushing him back from the rail. He staggered against the front of the pilot house. Forward, Emil Stone fired again, taking the glass out behind Lavery's head.

All this for a half-fare refund, Lavery thought. The packet was vibrating with maximum effort now. If she was going to

56

come out of the mud, this would do it. Something touched Lavery's shoulder as he saw Emil Stone trying to swing his gun up from behind a packing case and start forward again. Cole reached for the railing and discovered Captain Farrell's shortened rifle, handed out the window to him by the pilot clinging still, with his other hand, to the bucking wheel.

Cole was tired. The rifle seemed heavy. The darkness hid his sights. Stone seemed a long way away. But somehow Lavery got the heavy barrel up. Somehow he had a fleeting glimpse of a beefy, arrogant face in the notch of the sights. Somehow he managed a swift, steady pull on the trigger of the weapon. The jolt of the recoil drove him mercilessly back against the pilot house again. But Emil Stone rolled along the deck, trailing blood from the packing box behind which he had taken shelter across the grimy planking. Lavery staggered back to the rail.

Several of the passengers had drawn their weapons. And Spade Garrison had said something to them. They were loosely behind him. One of them called sharply to Cole: "Drop that rifle and come down off of there, brother! What in hell you trying to do?"

A small figure came rocking at a full run, hampered by swaying skirts, along the deck. She plowed into this man, wedging him against Spade Garrison. And her hand pointed to the dozen or so blacklegs who were piling through the last stretch of brush between them and the prow of the *Missouri Pride*.

"Wait till they're aboard, you fool! They'll tell you . . . while they're emptying your pockets!"

The man blinked. And at the same time, Marta Strand started up the ladder to the upper deck, deliberately putting her body in the line of fire between Cole Lavery and Garrison. She was on the second step of the ladder when the *Missouri Pride* shuddered heavily, smoothed, and a widening strip of water appeared between the brush into which her bow had been jammed and her forward rail. The men ashore, scant yards short of their goal, halted uncertainly.

Spade Garrison wheeled to the rail. "Run for it, you fools!" he bellowed. "It's shallow. You can damn' well wade it. If you can't swim!"

The passenger who had ordered Lavery down snapped out an oath and wheeled toward Garrison. "Senator . . . by hell, those are your men, aren't they?"

Garrison took an angry half step toward the man, checked himself, and suddenly launched himself over the rail. He landed heavily in the water. Two or three on deck opened up half-heartedly on him, but he worked into brush and vanished. Those ashore who had raced toward the packet now dived into cover. Cole thought it was all right. He thought everything was all right. Marta Strand came up over the head of the ladder. Lavery started toward her and spilled into a great void of space.

Lavery stayed aboard the *Missouri Pride* until all of her passengers had disembarked. He had not wanted thanks, and after a meeting on deck the men and women on the packet had been generous with gratitude in cash. He had a bad leg and a torn shoulder, but he had a stake. He supposed that was important. And he had made the kind of a beginning he wanted. There was only one other thing. Waiting in Captain Farrell's cabin, he began to be afraid Marta Strand had left with the others. Finally footfalls came along the deck, the latch turned back, and she came in.

"The pilot has told the whole story, Cole," she said. "Captain Farrell and Garrison planned the whole thing rather cleverly, didn't they? I'll never know how you guessed what they really intended."

"I didn't," Cole said dryly. "If I had, I wouldn't have these holes in me."

"There's a man from the United States Marshal's office coming aboard to see you in a little while. They're short of men out here. Are you going to listen to him, Cole?"

"I don't know," he said. "What are you going to do?"

"I don't know, either. Maybe I'll stay in Westport. Maybe I'll go farther West with a wagon train before I stop. Why?"

Cole had an answer to this question. But he also had some wounds that had to heal. He was also in a strange country where he had no roots. He had no plans for himself. How could he plan for another? He changed the answer. The West was wide. There was a lot of room to meet again.

"I wanted to see you some more," he said quietly.

Marta seemed to understand. She nodded.

"I'll be looking for you, Cole," she said. "Laramie, maybe. Or Fort Bridger or Fort Hall. Or Cherry Creek. Or the Smoky Hill. This has been a beginning. A good one. I'm glad you haven't tried to make it an end . . . for us. Maybe when we've found where our trails are going, whether they'll cross . . . maybe, sometime. . . ."

"Sure," Cole agreed. "Sometime."

He raised his arms. Marta bent over him. It was like the river, like the unbroken grass, like the fire of sunsets. He released her slowly. She smiled at him, turned, and went out the door. Cole drew a deep and steady breath.

He thought he knew where he was going now. A man would have to do a lot of building before he had something worth giving to a woman like this. And there was room to build as big as he wanted beyond the Missouri.

59

Commission Man

The author sent "Commission Man", the second Cole Lavery story, to his agent on January 15, 1948. It was sent on to Mike Tilden at Popular Publications who bought the story for *New Western*. Unlike *Dime Western* and *Star Western* at Popular Publications, *New Western*'s top rate was only .023¢ a word. The author was paid $202.40. Mike Tilden retitled the story "Jump-Off to Prairie Hell" when it appeared in *New Western* (6/48). Its title has been restored.

I

Cole Lavery swung down the rickety wooden steps fronting Mrs. Gimble's boarding house on the second street back from the waterfront in Westport Landing. He was still faintly unsteady and the sun had an unfamiliar feel against his face. There were two freshly healed bullet wounds in his body, neither of which he could begrudge. Both had been garnered in a little unpleasantness with steamboat bandits on the upriver trip from St. Louis, but the reward contributed by passengers after that affair had provided him with a stake, so that the wounds and the enforced inactivity at Mrs. Gimble's after his landing had been worthwhile, in their way, after all.

Turning down the street from the boarding house, Lavery began to walk more steadily as he realized how good his freedom felt and his healed wounds did not trouble him. He had two things uppermost in his mind. One was the expansion of the slender stake in his wallet into something more substantial. The second was a girl. A diminutive, independent girl named Marta Strand, who had sung for her supper on the riverboat and who had landed at Westport with the West before her and the spirit to tackle it.

Lavery had spent time with this girl on the riverboat. They had agreed to see each other ashore. Yet in spite of the fact she knew he had been wounded and in spite of the fact Mrs. Gimble's boarding house was not a hard one to find, she had not come looking for him. Now Lavery was determined to find her and find out why this was so. Women were scarce in Westport Landing. Women like Marta Strand were scarce the world over. He wanted to locate her before some arrogant devil in buckskin or a wealthy trader or a solid and honest emigrant offered her the kind of life for which she was looking.

Deliberately passing up two or three disreputable taverns along the muddy banks of the river, Lavery turned into a large establishment in fresh paint and good repair that boasted entertainment. Even at midday it was filled with a raucous crowd. The high pitch of voices speculating upon the unknown out on the grass and the smell of prodigious labor were in the air. Westport was the funnel through which the vast tide of California immigration was pouring, headstrong and reckless, ill-informed and friendless, drawn powerfully and too often disastrously by the lodestone of American River gold. The flavor of the tide was in this room. Confidence men, open thieves, and 100 other conniving leeches moved through the wagon men, bleeding them often without their knowledge.

Lavery thought of his own position here—his own determination reached while he lay in enforced helplessness at Mrs. Gimble's. He was as much a pilgrim as any man in this landing; he was as much fired with the restless knowledge that fortune lay for some, at least, beyond the plains. But there was a strong strain of practicality in him. And he had had opportunity to think at leisure, which many had not. There was a colossal folly in venturing immediately upon arrival out onto the grass. This was a new world, without restraints or law, in which men lived by patterns known nowhere else in the country. Often to survive and certainly to make the best of opportunity, a man should learn these patterns before attempting to live by them.

It had struck Lavery that the most noteworthy thing he had seen was the few places a puzzled emigrant could turn, here at the frontier, for information and advice on problems he did not understand. Where to buy what and how much to pay for it. The reputation of a wagon master who offered to captain a train for a fee. The best stock for wagons and for riding on the long Pacific trek. What to do in case of theft. How to forward mail. Mrs. Gimble knew Westport well, and Lavery had talked much with her. He had compiled a list of information. He thought he could discover more as he needed it. And he believed he knew how to increase his stake—once he had found Marta Strand.

There was a small stage at the far end of the tavern he had entered. A battered melodeon sat on this. A banjo leaned against an empty chair. A patched, incomplete set of traps was grouped about another. But the entertainers, questionably such, were not in evidence. Lavery shouldered to a place at the crowded bar, ordered a drink from the bartender, and, when it was set before him, he detained the man.

"I'm looking for a girl," he said. He indicated a head height against his chest. "About so tall. Sings kind of nice. Landed with a trunk full of singing clothes about three weeks ago. Just might have tried a place like this."

The barkeeper shook his head. "No girls here," he said. "Costs too much. Every time we get a woman on that stage, more damned furniture gets busted. Can't afford to run girls. Got more business than we can handle now."

Lavery peeled off a bill from the thin roll in his pocket. The barkeep brought back his change. He left a coin on the bar. The man picked it up with a look of surprise, pocketed it, and leaned toward him.

"Only one place to look for a girl in Westport, stranger," he said confidentially. "We couldn't hire one straight off a boat if we wanted. We'd have to go to Ben Carrick. Any girl that gets a job in this stinking town has got to do the same, sooner or later."

"Where do I find this Carrick?"

"At the Plantation," the barkeep said. "But don't be too inquisitive. The Saint don't like gents with a lot a questions about one of his girls."

"Who?"

"The Saint . . . Ben Carrick."

"A damned funny name."

"Won't seem so when you've seen him," the barkeep said flatly.

Lavery nodded thanks and backed away from the bar.

It wasn't hard to locate the Plantation. It was a large clapboard affair on a knoll behind the town. The front was painted a garish yellow and a couple of askew false columns supporting a flimsy entablature struggled to create an impression of Southern elegance and hospitality. The balance of the building, sides and back, was unadorned and unpainted, achieving a particular ugliness reserved for cheap siding long exposed to the weather. When Lavery reached the door of the place, a slovenly servant answered his knock. Gin smell was on his breath.

"We's closed," he growled. "Don't open till sunset."

"Sure," Lavery agreed slyly. "I don't want in. Just tell Miss Marta I've come to take her for the ride I promised. . . ."

The doormen's eyes rounded. "You promised Miss Marta a ride?" he protested. "You're crazy, boss. She ain't seen anybody since she got here. . . ."

The doorman broke off, shouldered aside by another figure. A tall man with a powerful body, a huge head, and a strangely serene, peaceful face.

"There's nobody here by the name of Marta," he said smoothly. "I'm sorry. . . ."

"No, you're not," Lavery said sharply. "You're lying. I'm looking for Marta Strand and your man just let it slip she's in your place."

The big man looked faintly pained. He turned to the doorman and spoke in a soft, gently chiding tone. "Rufus, your mouth is too big." The man smiled, a disarming expression, but Lavery didn't miss the way the doorman cringed. The big man turned back to Lavery. "You misunderstood," he said pleasantly. "I'm sorry."

Lavery felt the wicked strength of the man, belied by his features. Something was wrong that Marta Strand was here. She didn't belong in a place run by this smooth-faced giant.

"You're lying," he repeated stonily.

The big man shrugged and stepped back out of the doorway. "You require a lot of persuasion, friend," he complained mildly. "Come in, then. Rufus will take care of you."

Lavery stepped through the doorway. He didn't understand in time. The big man kicked the door closed behind him and swung rapidly away down the central hall. Lavery had only time to swing one arm in partial defense before the doorman waded into him. The fellow was skilled in his work and evidently anxious to make up for his earlier mistake. He worked with incredible swiftness and efficiency. One big fist struck Lavery low. The other straightened him as he bent. And he was hammered against the wall with a series of hard, jolting body blows.

Stunned, hurt, and explosively angry, but momentarily helpless, Lavery heard the door swing open. The doorman slammed a parting jolt hard under his ear and gave him a powerful shove. He staggered against one of the askew colonnades, lost his balance, and spilled into the dust at the foot of the steps. The door slammed above him. He rose slowly, slapped the dust from his knees, and wiped a trickle of blood from the corner of his mouth.

He was, he thought, going to be his own first customer. He had about time to get his new shingle hung over the office he had hired on the main street of the landing before the Plantation opened its doors for the night traffic. And when it did, he would be back.

II

Mrs. Gimble had been efficient in her performance of the errands her boarder had set her the past week. The sign painter had a burlap-wrapped bundle ready for Lavery when he called for it. When Lavery had paid him, the man scowled curiously.

"Ma Gimble said you'd stopped a couple slugs on a steamer," he said. "One of 'em hit you in the head?"

Puzzled, Lavery told the man no. The sign painter grinned, then, at his own humor. He indicated the bundle under Lavery's arm.

"Just wondered," he said. "That's the damnedest shingle I ever painted. Got the spelling of your name written down on the wall. Calculate I'll need it directly. Probably be painting up a headboard for 'em to plant over you."

Lavery grinned in answer.

"Like anybody else in Westport, I work on commissions," he said. "And I'll pay commissions to those that earn them. Send me some business and I'll make it worth your while."

The sign painter eyed him with a touch of grudging respect, his features sobering.

"I might do that," he said. "I might do just that. . . ."

Moving up the street, Lavery tried his key in the door of the little office Mrs. Gimble had rented for him. It fitted. There was a desk inside, a pair of chairs, a calendar, and a mirror—faithful rendition of his orders. Ma Gimble, he thought, had earned a commission herself. He found a nail in the exterior siding and hung his shingle. Backing onto the walk, he eyed it analytically.

COLE LAVERY
Information, Answers, and Service
For Emigrants and Pilgrims
I cure trouble. Try me.
(on Commission)

A man who had been standing on the opposite side of the street walked across unhurriedly and eyed the sign.

"Bill Ball does a nice job of lettering, don't he?" the man inquired.

Lavery looked at him. He was older, mature, a quiet sort of man without much about him to remember. Lavery nodded assent to his question.

"Trouble," the man said reflectively, "is sometime tolerably hard to cure."

"You want to talk to me?" Lavery asked with some sharpness.

The man nodded. "Could be," he agreed.

Lavery stepped into the office and kicked the two chairs around. He dropped into one of them. The man took the other.

"There isn't much law out here in the Territories," he said thoughtfully. "A man's sort of on his own. Trouble is, there ain't too many coming up the river these days who can swing their own pick. It's costing pilgrims twice what it should to get wagons and equipment for the crossing ahead of them. That's bad. Most of them aren't any too well heeled as it is, and, when their money'll only buy half what it should, it means a lot of them are heading across the grass to break their hearts. It ought to be different."

"I figured I'd buy for those that wanted me to," Lavery said. "I had questions asked around town and I aim to ask more. I think I can save my customers money."

"Don't doubt it," the man in the other chair agreed. "Right good idea you've got. Wish somebody'd had it sooner. Only thing is . . . that extra money that's being spent here is going into somebody's pocket. And when you start buying close for your customers, you're costing that somebody a lot of extra profit he's gotten used to. I doubt he's going to want you to stay in business."

"A man takes same chances," Lavery said.

"Ain't worth his salt if he won't," his visitor agreed seriously. "Point is, how smart is it for a gent with a couple of half-healed holes in him to pile the odds too high?"

"You trying to tell me something?" Lavery asked.

The man shook his head. "Not particularly," he said. "Just pointing out there's two sides to a fence. Wanted to be sure you'd seen both of them. I've got a respect for the law out here, such as it is. The law's got its problems. If it's on its toes, it's got as much interest in a dead man before he's killed as it has in him after he's nose down in the dust. Just thought I'd better have a word with you, Lavery. That's all."

Lavery snorted. "The reason I can do any business here is because there isn't any law. Being as this is a federal territory, there aren't any state officers . . . and Westport is a long way from Washington. What's your stake in the time you're taking with me?"

The man smiled a little at the acid in Lavery and parted his vest. The red light of the low sun, spilling through the door of the office, glinted momentarily on a brightly burnished badge.

"I'm Jeff Peterson, of the United States Marshal's office," the man said quietly. "In a way I suppose you might say I'm what law there is in Westport. I'm just being neighborly, Lavery. Thought you ought to be warned to watch yourself. That sign'll get you business . . . and it'll get you trouble. Wanted you to know, if you run into something a little out of your line, I might give you a hand."

Lavery eased. He was astonished. This quiet man with his slow way of speech was faced with a towering problem. But Jeff Peterson's manner indicated he was capable of handling it as he spoke—unhurriedly and without uproar. Rising, Lavery offered the man his hand.

"Forgive the sparks, Marshal," he said. "I'm pleased to meet you. It isn't on my sign, but if the law needs help here,

I'm handy and willing. The quicker this country starts thinking of land and sweat again, instead of top odds on every roll of the dice and California gold, the quicker its going to amount to something."

"That's a fact." Peterson nodded. He moved to the doorway and turned. "Just thinking, Lavery . . . the Saint . . . Ben Carrick, you know . . . has stacked up just a little too high for me to tackle yet. And my badge lets me tackle some sizeable *hombres*. I've been waiting till he's weaved himself plenty of rope. Patience tacks years onto a man's life. Thought you'd like to know that. Maybe you'll want to think of it a bit. Patience might pay off in your line, too."

"All right, Marshal," Lavery agreed. "I'll think about it."

Peterson waved his hand and moved along the walk.

Before daylight was entirely gone, a wagon man had come uncertainly in with a query as to where a man could buy a pair of good Missouri mules and a fresh milk cow with calf for a price a dirt farmer could afford to pay. Lavery had sold him the animals from a bunch owned by a cough-ridden tenant at Mrs. Gimble's who had given up the crossing of the plains he had intended and was selling out before he turned homeward. The wagon man had doubled Lavery's $10 commission when he learned the reasonable price he was asked to pay. It was fully dark on the street when Lavery came out onto the walk and locked his door for the night.

Suddenly hungry, Lavery paused in a small restaurant to eat. He felt tired. His first day away from Mrs. Gimble's had been long. And he was not yet done. He had a little business with a man named Ben Carrick.

Leaving the restaurant, he walked unhurriedly the length of the street and turned up one of the footpaths leading to the Plantation. As he did so, a man sauntered out of the shadows, a heavy gun in his hand. He thrust it impersonally into Lavery's belly. Lavery recognized Jeff Peterson.

"Boy, I tried to tell you," Peterson said wearily. "You ain't dry enough behind the ears to do what you're trying. I got a conscience. It says I can't let you plow out the furrow you're starting. Hand over your gun."

"What the hell is this, an arrest?" Lavery protested.

Peterson shook his head. "Can't arrest an honest man and I hope to hell you're honest . . . it pains me to beat the devil to make a mistake about a man." he said. "I'm just making sure that, if you go up to the Saint's place, you don't get reckless and make somebody put a bullet in you. There's a couple of jokers hang around the Saint who have done just that to a couple of nice, earnest, fire-eatin' pilgrims. I'm cheating 'em out of a chance with you."

"If the Plantation is the hell hole you paint it and you're the law, why don't you clean it out?" Lavery snapped unpleasantly.

Peterson continued to smile, untroubled. "Boy, you can't dry up the Missouri with a dish rag. Come on, the gun, now. Then you trot along up to the Saint's if you've a mind. But you better keep your tongue in your mouth. Save your getting another lump on your jaw to match the one you've got."

There was a strong compulsion in Peterson, in spite of his apparent mildness. Lavery reluctantly unhung his gun and passed it across. The marshal nodded pleasantly and stepped backward into the brush from which he had emerged. As he moved on up the path to Ben Carrick's place, Lavery thought that the man they called the Saint must be the exact opposite—complete with tail, horns, and fire in his nostrils. He had, at least, crested a lot of respect

70

for his flint in the office of the United States Marshal, and unwillingly. Still thinking of the girl with whom he had walked the deck of an upriver packet but remembering he was now unarmed, Cole Lavery walked more softly up the hill.

III

There was no one on duty at the door of the Plantation. It stood open and light flooded through it out onto the porticoed verandah. Brassy music, the beat of feet in heavy shoes, and the high talk of men at drink poured from it. Lavery entered without challenge.

One thing became immediately apparent. The Plantation was doing the biggest business in Westport. And this was paradoxical, since it was some distance from the main part of town and therefore more difficult of access, and because it was without a question the poorest tavern in the landing. The puncheon flooring was makeshift and in miserable condition. The bar was no more than hand-roughed planks, carelessly nailed to supports. The place was dirty and ill-kempt, and night river winds, moving along the bluffs, whistled through it uncomfortably. There was no attempt to cater to the trade in the place and it was curious that so much business came Carrick's way.

Lavery shouldered to the bar, ordered a drink, and had just lifted it, when he found an explanation. A small, ruddy man in better than usual gear stood a little distance from him. He seemed familiar and Lavery finally decided he was a man named Hennessey, who had a little money-changing and mail-forwarding business a few doors down the main street of town from Lavery's own new location. He seemed uneasy. Lavery saw he was watching the approach of a short, incredibly powerful man with a bullet head. The fellow was grinning and his easy familiarity with those among whom he moved was a plain indication he was a house man. He sidled in beside the townsmen and spoke softly.

"Good thing you showed up, Hennessey," he murmured. "I was afraid I'd have to come down to town after you."

"Hoping you would, you mean, Garrett," the money-changer said acidly. "I got your message. I'm here. What's up?"

"The boss doesn't like the way you're doing business. He's heard you've cut your rates. And he hasn't gotten a report from you in a week."

Hennessey glared at the man. "Charging a dollar out of ten for making small change out of big bills and gold out of paper and *vice versa* is too steep a cut," he said defensively. "These emigrants haven't got all the money in the world. I've got to leave them some. And I'm onto the reports of transactions I've been sending up here. Every time I report changing a big bill or a good chunk of gold for a man, he's found next morning down on the riverbank with a lump on his head and empty pockets. But Carrick has got no kick coming. I'm paying for the privilege of working in this town. I'm keeping careful records and he'll get his third of every commission I take in. If he wants any more, he can go to hell! You tell him. . . ."

Hennessey swung away from the bar. Garrett caught the front of his coat and pulled him back.

"You know better than that," the house man said pleasantly. "The Saint doesn't like that kind of talk. You got to learn a lesson, Hennessey, right out where everybody can see you. If you'll talk like that here, you've been doing it in town, too. Folks have got to understand that kind of talk don't pay. . . ."

There was absolutely no warning. Garrett's heavy fist crossed in a skidding impact that did a maximum of damage to Hennessey's face. A ruthless, spirit-breaking blow. Lavery, close, saw Garrett slip a knife from his own belt and drop it to the floor. Garrett found this with his toe and sent it skidding out into the room. Savagely the squat man forced Hennessey's limp body against the bar and drove half a dozen bone-crushing blows into his body. Then he released the man and let him slide to the floor. Hennessey was bleeding from the mouth and the nose. The crowd had fallen silent. Garrett stepped back from the bar, dusted his hands, and tilted his head toward the blade lying out on the puncheon.

"Pulled a knife on me," he said in bland explanation. He started moving away. Lavery knelt swiftly beside Hennessey. The man's coat was open, revealing a short, light gun in his vest. Lavery lifted it, knowing the man would have no immediate need for it. Straightening, he stepped after Garrett and caught his arm.

"I saw that . . . heard it," he said. "Set me thinking. I opened a commission office in the landing today. Maybe I better see your boss."

Garrett looked him over narrowly. "What's your name?" he asked.

"Cole Lavery."

Garrett nodded. "Maybe you better," he agreed. "Come on."

Lavery followed the man across the big main room and through a small door at the rear. This gave onto a narrow, steep stair. At the head of this was another door. Garrett opened the snap lock on this with a key. They stepped into a comfortable room, better furnished than any Lavery had seen since his arrival on the river. Garrett knocked on a door opposite. It opened in a moment and Ben Carrick came from his inner quarters. He glanced quickly from Lavery to Garrett.

"I just built a fire under Hennessey downstairs. This gent was close enough to get the drift. Spooked him some. He's just opened up in town and he figured he'd better talk to you. Name's Lavery."

The Saint nodded. "I've met Lavery," he said dryly. "This afternoon. What's on your mind now?"

"I understand you're taking a cut out of Hennessey's business. Thought you'd probably want a cut out of mine, too. I'd rather come talking to you than have my belly caved in by Garrett."

"Would you?" Ben Carrick asked. "I wonder about that, Lavery. Just what is your business in Westport?"

"Getting along," Lavery said flatly. "Right now, I do buying and selling, on commission. Tomorrow maybe it'll be something else."

The Saint nodded thoughtfully. "I got a line on you after you were here today," he said. "So you're a commission man. Maybe that's right. I hear you collected a little commission from the passengers of the *Missouri Pride* for saving their purses for them. But I tell you what I think. I think you're a damned reformer that can't keep his nose out of somebody else's business. And I don't like reformers. You're going to get out of Westport in a hurry, Lavery. I don't like you and I don't like the company you keep. I'm going to settle all of my business with you, right now. I don't want any part of your take. You misunderstood the Hennessey thing. He pulled a knife on Garrett, didn't he?

Fists against a knife is fair exchange. I run a tavern. That's all, a tavern. Get that straight and keep it straight. Don't try to make anything else out of it."

"I saw the knife," Lavery agreed, then added: "I saw it pulled."

Garrett scowled.

The Saint continued to eye Lavery in speculation. "I thought this afternoon you might be troublesome if you hung around the landing. I'm plenty right, apparently. You see too many things. You shouldn't have come back to the Plantation."

"I had good reason, Carrick," Lavery said quietly. "Pilgrims coming up the river aren't all alike. I had a notion you might interfere in the business I started today. And like I told you this afternoon, you've got something here I want."

"The girl, eh?" Carrick said. "All right, we'll have that out. You're so dammed sure you've got your initials chalked on her. Garrett, bring in Marta . . . that little hellcat from the *Missouri Pride*. . . ."

Garrett opened the door and stepped out.

The Saint smiled benignly. "And what makes you so damned sure I haven't interfered with the business you started this afternoon, Lavery?" he asked.

Before Lavery could pry at this, the door opened again. A disheveled girl came in angrily, followed by Garrett. The imprint of a small hand was on Garrett's cheek. The girl stormed across to Carrick.

"How much longer does this keep up?" she asked irately. "I tell you, I'll sing where I please, on the river or up it or under it, and you can keep me in this whitewashed excuse for a rat's nest till you've got whiskers to your knees and the answer will be the same!"

"Marta, my dear," Carrick said softly, "control yourself. You have company."

The girl wheeled toward Lavery. The same girl with whom he had walked one evening on the deck of the *Missouri Pride*. The girl who had admitted she was traveling upriver for the same reasons as Lavery himself. A search for what lay beyond the setting sun. A hope that somewhere west of the Big Muddy, where all beginnings were new, her roots would find the anchor they craved. A beautiful girl, all rich, strong whiskey, and slumbering fire—and promise, wonderful promise.

Lavery saw recognition, eagerness come up swiftly in her eyes. Then, as he started to speak, it died suddenly. The girl turned slowly back to Ben Carrick.

"Company . . . for me?" she asked harshly. "You're crazy."

"You don't know this man?"

"How long do you think my memory is?" the girl snapped. "Men are my living. Do I have to remember them all?"

Ben Carrick laughed. "Thank you, my dear girl," he said. "You've cleared up an unpleasant matter. . . ." He touched Marta Strand's shoulder with his hand. Her palm exploded against his cheek resoundingly and she strode rapidly back out the still open door. Garrett grinned briefly at the color suffusing Carrick's normally bland face, then ducked after the girl. Carrick scowled at Lavery.

"I can thank you for that," he said. "You can see well enough the girl doesn't even know you. It's time to start moving, Lavery. Tonight. Out of the landing. A long way out of it."

"You can thank your own wandering hand," Lavery said evenly. "And I'm too old to believe everything I see,

76

Carrick. We'll say you held the top cards this hand and let it go at that."

Carrick shrugged. "Stubborn men have bad hearts in this country," he murmured. "They just stop ticking."

"I'll remember to keep mine wound," Lavery said.

Turning, he left the room and clattered down the stairs. In the middle of the narrow passage, he met Garrett, on his way up. The man flattened against the wall to let him pass. Lavery paused an instant.

"There was a doorkeeper this afternoon," he said. "I want you to give him something for me."

Pivoting on the step, he slammed his fist in a short arc. Garrett's head snapped back against the wall. His eyes rolled and he sagged loosely. Lavery went on down the steps, closing the door at the bottom behind him.

IV

Coming into the main street of the landing, Lavery saw lights up fully at Mrs. Gimble's boarding house. He suddenly felt almost overpoweringly weary and he paused, wanting to turn in and climb the stairs and hit the hay. But he knew that, if he did, he would be delaying his thinking. And there were things that had to be thought out tonight. He swung on down the street, reaching the door of his office in a few moments. He fitted his key and stepped in. Belatedly he realized that, when he had sent Ma Gimble out to shop for furnishings, he had neglected to remind her of a lamp. He shrugged. It was all right, for now. He could think even better in the darkness. He kicked the door closed. As he did so, Jeff Peterson's voice sounded from the corner behind it.

"I want to see you hang, Lavery," the marshal said quietly. "Don't make me cut you down."

Lavery stood carefully without moving.

"What are you talking about?" he snapped.

"Why, I'll tell you," Peterson said imperturbably. "Directly . . . directly."

The officer moved silently close. His swift hand located the small gun Lavery had picked up in the main room of the Plantation. It made a wooden sound as Peterson dropped it into the drawer of Lavery's desk. A chair skidded on the flooring. Lavery felt the edge of it press against the inside of his knees.

"Sit down, Lavery," Peterson went on. "We're going to have a long talk."

Lavery dropped onto the chair and twisted around. The marshal was behind his own desk, lolling back a little in his chair and the bland, easy, unhurried friendliness that had earlier marked the man was gone from features now plain enough in the half darkness of the unlighted room. Peterson was frigidly angry. He was condemning. And he was triumphant.

"You rooked me, son," he said. "I came close to stacking my chips all with you. The Saint moved too fast or I'd have been with you, blind."

"What the hell are you talking about?" Lavery demanded again.

Peterson smiled wearily. "Laws make the lawless," he said. "Not because they set up rules for somebody to break, but because they set up rules that officers have got to stick to. If I could work hunches . . . if I could put iron on the gents I don't like, just because I don't like them and because I'm guessing they're dealing off the bottom . . . I'd have an easy job. The thing is . . . I got to remember a court has got to have evidence. I've got to assume even the devil is wearing a clean shirt till I can prove otherwise. I've been working on what the trouble in the landing is for weeks. And all of the time I've known it's been Ben Carrick. But I didn't have any way to prove he was biting a little meat out of every piece of business in town and landing hard on them that didn't play his game. Carrick knew I was after him, and he was laughing. Dead men don't tell who killed them."

"My name is Lavery. You're talking about Carrick."

"I'm talking about you!" Peterson said sharply. "You did a little business about nightfall. Sounded like nice, clean business when I heard of it. A fair deal to both sides. No cut out for Carrick. Made me happy. That's why I took your gun. Wanted you alive tomorrow to do some more. The landing needs that kind of business, and I figured you couldn't get into killing trouble with the Saint if you weren't armed. Then, while you're up talking to your boss, I saw how it really was. The man who bought them mules and the man who sold them didn't want to pay the kind of cut Carrick's been demanding. You couldn't get it for him. So you run up to tell him about it. And Carrick takes care of those two clients of yours that were stubborn."

Lavery braced himself. He remembered a smoothly mocking question Ben Carrick had asked him: *And what makes you so damned sure I haven't interfered in the business you did this afternoon, Lavery?*

"What happened?" he asked Jeff Peterson.

"Want me to tell you your name, too?" the marshal asked acidly. "You'll be pretending you don't know it next. The sick man at Ma Gimble's who sold the mules through you was clubbed down in Ma's front yard and his pockets emptied of his take. He was clubbed too hard. He's going to die. And the wagon man who bought the mules was found dead in his own supper fire, a bullet into the back of his head from the shadows while he was cooking his meal. Warning from Ben Carrick and young Lavery that buyer and seller in the landing have got to pay the commission that's asked . . . or else. What I've got ain't evidence, Lavery, but I can play rough, too. You're going to talk, and it's going to be where there's a federal judge handy to listen. You and me are taking a night boat down the river . . . and Ben Carrick's going to be with us, in irons. You're both going to hang."

"You haven't got Carrick," Lavery pointed out.

Jeff Peterson smiled grimly. "No," he agreed. "But I've got you. And I didn't have any trouble at it. You think I can't snag the Saint, too?"

Lavery looked at the peace officer. His very quiet plainness had something implacable in it. The man was wholly without fear. His judgment was sure, his inclination to be certain of details. But when the last chips were down, Jeff Peterson could claw a high mark on any tree.

"No," Lavery said slowly. "I think you'd try, all right, and alone, at that. And maybe, if the breaks are right, you'll get him. But you haven't got enough on him and bucking the set-up at the Plantation isn't a one-man job. You better listen to me."

Peterson eased in his chair and nodded somberly. "Go ahead," he agreed. "I told you you'd have to talk. If you do it now, it'll save some rough handling later."

Lavery leaned forward earnestly and briefly sketched what had happened at the Plantation. He went on to add his own conviction that the marshal's estimate of Carrick's operations was correct. He cited Carrick's attitude toward himself and the affair of Garrett and Hennessey at the bar in the place as additional proof. He said nothing about Marta Strand, since the whole matter of the girl was not clear in his own mind. He knew that she remembered him. She had to. And her first outburst in Carrick's quarters had proved how desperately she hated the set-up at the Plantation. It had been, in fact, positive proof that she was being held unwillingly. Why she had not taken advantage of his own implied offer of help was the puzzling thing. When he was finished, Peterson frowned.

"It's no use, Lavery," he said flatly. "I'm sorry as hell you're mixed up in this. I figured you as a boy I could get to turn a hand with me when the pull got steep. And I'm going to need a hand . . . all I can get. But you tell this too smooth. You haven't admitted the real reason you went up to see Carrick. That don't do you no good. Might as well tell me you went up to see one of Carrick's girls. That'd hold about as much water as this yarn you've told me."

Peterson's stubbornness chafed roughly across Lavery's anger, yet there was the sobering thought that from the officer's point of view solid reasoning backed him up. Lavery felt like a fool, knowing what else he could say would only add to the man's conviction of rightness in his charge against Cole Lavery, but the rest of the story had to come out.

"There *is* a girl up there, Marshal," he said quietly. "That is why I went up to the Plantation both times. A girl I met on the *Missouri Pride*, coming upriver. A girl I want to see again and one that wants to see me. She's there, all right. Carrick's holding her. And she doesn't like it. That's why I've got to go back again."

Peterson laughed. "I'll say this, Lavery, you're a hard man to discourage. I call your next move and you make it, anyway. . . ." Peterson broke off suddenly. Steps had come softly, swiftly along the walk outside of the darkened office. They halted for a moment outside the door.

There was a rustle of movement. A shadow was apparent

through the small glass in the door. Both Peterson and Lavery plunged silently toward the floor, thinking how easily a bullet could come through the pane. Lavery was closest to the door. He saw the slip of white paper appear under it and slide out onto the floor. The steps outside hurried swiftly on. Lavery rose to his knees and reached for the envelope. Peterson stepped past him, pinned his reaching hand down, and lifted it himself. Both men stood up and backed to the chairs.

With a quick glance at his prisoner, Peterson tore open the envelope, snapped a match alight, and hastily read its contents. The match flickered and died. Peterson swore softly.

"I'll say this, Lavery," he murmured, "when you give a man a story, you sure go the whole way, timing and all, to make it look real. Here. . . ."

He passed the note across. Lavery snapped the paper out flat and kindled his own match. The message he read was brief:

Cole Lavery:

Forgive me for what happened in Carrick's office. I hear things here and had to do that for you. You've been seen in town with a man known to be from the Marshal's Office. Carrick and Garrett are afraid of you. Get out of town tonight. Tomorrow will be too late. I'll be all right. A friend is delivering this. At the first chance, she'll help me escape, too. Wait for me up the trail.

Marta

When Lavery's match went out, Jeff Peterson scraped his boots across the floor.

"I dislike making a mistake about a man one way as the other, Lavery," he said slowly. "I've got sense enough to see that you couldn't have known I would be waiting here for you. You couldn't have rigged it up at the Plantation to have this note sent down just at this minute to haul you out of a tight. Instead of your being smeared up with Carrick, it looks to me like you've got painted with my brush. I think the girl's right. You've got to get out of town tonight . . . and not down the river in irons, like I promised, either."

"And leave Marta up there?" Lavery asked harshly.

Peterson grinned widely. "I didn't figure you would," he admitted. "Still a peace officer has got his duty and mine was to give you the best damned advice I could. Only way to get that girl is to go back up the knoll. And climbing those paths for either one of us is like getting a short ticket to hell punched out in advance."

"You want Carrick," Lavery reminded the man.

Peterson nodded. "Carrick and this Garrett you were talking about," he agreed. "And tonight . . . before they figure their toes are being stood on in some other deal and they plow somebody else under."

"What are we waiting for, then?" Lavery asked.

Peterson stood up and reached into a hip pocket, under the tail of his coat. "Here, boy," he said. "Here's your own gun. You'll do better with it than with that little popgun you borrowed from Phil Hennessey."

At the foot of the path leading up the knoll from town to Ben Carrick's Plantation, Jeff Peterson paused.

"I've looked the place over pretty carefully, Lavery," he said. "There's a stair from the main room up to Carrick's office. I'll find him there. The girl you're looking for will be in one of the back rooms on the second floor of the place and there's a back way in. I don't know just how it goes, but the regular girls at Carrick's seem to use it. Apparently he keeps those he's persuading to pay him a hiring commission up there, too. The way I see it, we'll split about here. You cut for the back and get the girl free. There'll be some ruckus over that. It'll give me a diversion . . . it'll draw some attention. That ought to pull the odds down about right."

"You can't arrest Ben Carrick and Garrett in their own place single-handed, Peterson," Lavery protested.

The marshal dropped a hand onto his shoulder. "Son, I've been in this business quite a spell. One reason I've been able to stay in it is that I've learned things. Violence makes a country. A people that has been through a lot of hell together somehow eventually manage to build something pretty good out of their experiences. And where's there's violence, the law has got to sort of make its own pattern. It isn't what's in the statute books that is important out here now. What really counts is that little fellows like you and Hennessey and the emigrants have the freedom to do what they want within reason. Protecting that freedom is why the statute books were written and protecting that freedom is my job. I don't expect to arrest either Ben Carrick or his man Garrett. I'm not fool enough to think for a minute they'd stand for that. They'd resist if I tried. I'm anticipating that. So the best I can do is put them out of business . . . if my luck holds."

"We'll take the front door together," Lavery said quietly. "That'll stack better odds than anything I might do out back. I came out to this country. I expect something from it. I'm not a fool, either. Nobody gets something for nothing. I've got to give. Siding you seems as good a way as any other."

Jeff Peterson nodded. "Sure," he agreed. "That's the feeling that does the building . . . that giving a little. More and more of the emigrants are beginning to see it. That means a couple, three years will see a lot of settlement here on the river. A preacher'll want to give and there'll be a church. A good medico will forget about his fees and we'll have tolerable medicine. Women will give, and they'll makeshift till there's actually homes right here in the landing. After that, milled lumber and shingles and lace curtains will come fast. And somebody'll give time at practically no pay for a school. But you're trying to give too damned much. This is my job. You've got yours. That girl is hoping high you'll spring her out of Ben Carrick's place. You stick to that."

The officer's voice was too firm for further argument. Lavery shrugged and gripped the other's hand for a moment. He started to swing away. Peterson checked him.

"You're in business, boy, and a businessman has got to get ahead. I want you should have a commission off of this. Ma Gimble, at the place you board, has been holding five hundred dollars in gold . . . government money . . . for me in case I needed to post a reward. I want you should have it. Tell her if I don't get a chance. A man setting himself up with a girl runs short of cash almighty quick. And you'll have earned it."

Lavery shook his head. "I figure Carrick and Garrett have bought this trouble," he said. "And when I hung out my shingle, I made it policy that the buyer would always pay my fee. Keeps the seller from adding it to his price and chasing prices way up. What I've got coming, I'll collect at the Plantation."

Lavery swung on, then, carrying wide of the front of the tavern above him in order to approach it from the rear.

Near the crest of the knoll he looked back. Peterson had waited a few moments before starting up the hill. Lavery thought the man would reach the front door at about the same time as he reached the one in back. Satisfied, he moved on.

Peterson had told him that the door was in the center of the rear wall of the place. Lavery noted that a row of windows in the floor about it were barred with straps of iron— perhaps a safeguard for those who leaned from them when they were open, but effective, also, to imprison those who might otherwise climb through them and risk a drop to the ground.

The door was locked, but the fastening appeared to be a wrought-iron affair, common in the landing and similar to that on Lavery's own office door. He fitted his own un- complicated, bulky key into the slot and turned it sharply. The single tumbler within *clicked* over, and, when he turned the knob, the door swung open. Checking the set of his gun in its holster, Lavery stepped across a short hall outside of what was apparently the kitchen of the Plantation and took the stairs reaching up from it at a fast, light step.

Another hall headed the second-floor landing. Numerous doors opened off of this. Two were fastened on the hall side with hasp, staple, and padlock. The hall was empty. Lavery stopped in front of the first locked door. The lock was a heavy affair. He listened for a moment. There seemed an unusual stir in the lower front part of the building. He thought Jeff Peterson must have already stepped into the bar. The suspicion was immediately con- firmed by the flat explosion of a pistol fired within walls. Time was short.

Using the barrel of his gun for a hammer, Lavery swung a sharp blow against the lock in front of him. A rivet pulled free, and the hoop sprang open. He disengaged it from the staple, snapped the hasp back, and kicked the door open. A thin, wild-eyed girl, flat-chested, terrifiedly young, stared at him across a bed, behind which she crouched.

"Let me go!" she screamed. "I've changed my mind. I don't want to sing. I don't want to dance. I want to go back to the wagons. That's all. The train is leaving in the morning. I want to go back to Dad. . . ."

"Then move." Lavery snapped. "Your door's open and so's the one at the bottom of the stairs. Fast, now!"

The girl stared in disbelief, then darted across the room and slid past.

"Where's Marta Strand?" Lavery asked sharply.

The frightened girl ignored him, making no answer. Barefooted she ran down the rough pine stairs. But there was an answer to his query. His name, called fearfully from behind the other locked door, followed by the quick drum of fists against the inside of the panel. At the same instant came the opening of another door at the far end of the dogleg hall and the drum of heavy feet in a full run toward him.

Leaping forward, Lavery swung at the second lock. It was stubborn. On the second stroke it shattered. With fingers that seemed deliberately slow of their own stubborn accord, he freed the hasp. The door swung back. He had a momentary glimpse of Marta Strand, soft-eyed with welcome as she had been the last time he had seen her aboard the *Missouri Pride*. Then a gun shook the hall and a great gouge of fresh pine wiped across the sill almost beside his cheek. He wheeled. The doorman who had mauled him the first trip up this knoll was crouched at the bend of the hall, steadying a huge pistol against the framing.

It was a swift, unconsidered, awkward shot. Lavery was

pleased. He had tried to learn the hang and balance of a gun in his own hills before he had started up the river, knowing he would need such knowledge. He had tried to convert the fair accuracy of a hunter into the quick and ready speed of a man who used a gun for defense. But such skill took time in learning. He appeared to have learned well. His bullet hit the doorman somewhere high in the torso and slammed him backward to the floor.

"Out . . . the back way," Lavery grunted to Marta Strand. "My office . . . where you sent the note to me in town tonight. I'll see you there."

Without waiting for an answer, he sprinted down the hall, leaping over the fallen man, and skidded around the dogleg turn. A heavy door faced him. It wasn't locked. Beyond it he could hear rising tumult. Gunfire had broken out in ragged, staccato rhythm, apparently centered beyond this panel. He jerked the door open and found himself in the tiny, square hall at the head of the narrow stairs that led from the main room of the Plantation to Ben Carrick's quarters.

The lower door was open. Curious faces were tilted up the stairs. These ducked out of sight as Lavery appeared. A gun sounded again in the direction of Carrick's quarters. Lavery crossed the hall in a stride and kicked open the door through which he had earlier passed to face the Saint.

The room beyond was deserted and another door gaped open. Three men were in the rich sleeping room beyond it. Jeff Peterson, apparently only a moment before flung there, was sprawled half dazedly into a corner. The marshal was clutching a bullet-torn forearm and his eyes were bitterly on a weapon that lay on the floor two yards from him. As Lavery's rush carried him farther into the room, he saw a fourth man, also on the floor. A limply sprawled figure collapsed on his drawn gun. A man he didn't know. Beyond this man, coolly drawn up against the wall and smiling faintly over the length of hickory with which he had evidently just knocked Peterson down stood Ben Carrick.

Lavery didn't see Garrett, crouched to one aide of the door, quite in time. The man rose, his pistol high, and chopped it down. Lavery swung his head clear, but the dropping blow caught him on the crown of his shoulder with paralyzing force. He reeled, lost his footing, and went to one knee. Clumsily, with a tantalizing slowness, he shifted his gun from his numbed right hand to his unfamiliar left, knowing the while that Garrett, dropping his weapon into line for a clean shot, would have a bullet into him before he could half raise his weapon.

For this single instant, Lavery understood the look in Jeff Peterson's eyes. A look half of condemnation and half of gratitude. Peterson knew that Carrick would see them both dead. Garrett's gun would fire twice. In the morning, business would progress as usual at the Plantation. In the morning Ben Carrick would again be boss of every transaction in the landing. There could not even be too many questions about the whereabouts of a federal marshal and a pilgrim who had turned commission man for a few hours. People learned fast, faced with violence. And they'd know Ben Carrick wanted no questions. So they'd drawn their cards and hadn't filled the hand they'd tried to play. Jeff Peterson's look said these things. It said that Cole Lavery was a fool, but a man to ride the river with. It said this wasn't death that faced them, but defeat. It was the defeat that was important. For it was the defeat of peace and prosperity for Westport, at the same time.

Lavery braced himself against the coming of Garrett's shot. But suddenly the man was obscured by a rush of smoke from the doorway. His squat, powerful body was flung roughly against the wall. It clung there for a moment, as though by adhesion of its own. Then fell heavily. And Marta Strand staggered into the room.

The girl was holding the heavy gun that the doorman in the rear hallway had fired at Lavery firmly clutched in both of her small hands. Her eyes were wide with fear of the thing she was doing and her color was gone. But Lavery saw her thumbs clawing frantically at the heavy hammer. Ben Carrick saw this, too—this and the fact the muzzle of the weapon was holding unsteadily on him. He roared suddenly, a jarring rush of sound, and lunged across the room toward the girl, his length of hickory axe handle held high.

In Carrick's hand, the weapon was a lethal one. The power in his body behind that bludgeon could have dropped a bull buffalo. Marta Strand looked fragile before him. Lavery shook off his daze. He had to be so very sure with his unfamiliar left hand. He had to be so very fast. Faster than he had ever guessed there would be need. He was certain that the shot was too late—that Carrick's club could crush the girl's head when his weapon fired. Carrick's lunge continued, but he went past the girl with no effort to complete the swing of his club, and crashed into the wall. He rebounded unsteadily from this, turned himself with the stubbornness of a dying will, and walked a step out into the room again before he collapsed.

Jeff Peterson pulled himself painfully to his feet, holding his injured arm out from him with his good hand so that the slow drip of blood would not foul his clothing. He looked at Marta Strand.

"Talk about saints!" he said to Lavery.

"My partner," Lavery said. "Starting right now. M. and C. Lavery . . . we aim to please."

"Yeah, on commission," Peterson added with dry humor.

Color was coming back into Marta's cheeks. She looked around for a place to put the heavy gun in her hands, then shrugged with a quick smile, and dropped it on the floor. She crossed to Lavery.

"Cole . . . I didn't want you to come up here, but I was afraid you wouldn't," she said quietly. "Cole . . . I . . . I. . . ."

Lavery grinned and nodded. "Yeah, me, too," he said. "I'll collect from Jeff tomorrow for this chore. Anyhow, I didn't climb this knoll for him. It was on account of you. And when a job's done, I expect to get paid. . . ."

The girl's head tilted back. Lavery's arms closed around her. He had thought what this would be like, back on the *Missouri Pride*. Now he knew. And he decided he had a hell of a feeble imagination. Peterson was crazy. It wasn't sand and bucking the tigers and the coming of 10,000 wagons that built a country out of a frontier. The building was done like this. He kissed the girl. After a moment, Marta pushed him away.

"The firm will be a success, Cole," she said softly. "We'll always show a profit if you're going to be so greedy on every commission you collect."

Jeff Peterson chuckled. "Lady, it isn't that he's greedy. He just likes the wampum you pay off with. Come on, let's get out of here."

Wagon Boss

Tom W. Blackburn titled the third Cole Lavery story "White Collar Wagon Boss" when he sent it to the August Lenniger Literary Agency on March 2, 1948. Lenniger was of the opinion that the story was of such quality that it should be sent to Rogers Terrill, editor of Popular Publications' slick magazine, *Argosy*. Terrill bought the story on April 18, 1948 and the author was paid $816.75 at this magazine's higher word rate of .099¢. Terrill didn't want the story to be connected to the Cole Lavery series that had been appearing in various Popular Publications pulp magazines, so he changed the names of Cole Lavery and Marta Lavery to Court Lansing and Martha Lansing. The titled was shortened to "Wagon Boss" upon publication in *Argosy* (10/48). The magazine title has been retained for the story's appearance here, although the names of the principals have been changed back to Cole and Marta Lavery.

I

Near sunset, Cole Lavery came up from the tail of the train. One pocket of his coat bulged with a notebook containing ominous notations. The Ferris wagon had a cracked hub; two days of rolling left in it, no more. Two of the Mallory kids were sick, one of them dangerously so. The Cosgrove cow, one of the two fresh animals in the train, had stepped into a prairie dog hole. Lavery himself had been forced to shoot it. Cosgrove, for all his heavy-handed bluffing, could beat his wife but he couldn't kill the cow. The Kane woman, shunned by the other wives because of some doubt as to the validity of the marriage she claimed with Kane, was approaching labor. Lavery thought Kane looked bad.

There wasn't a sound span of draft animals among the wagons. All were spent from too much traveling, from a desperate attempt to cover too many miles in too short a time.

Lavery pulled up at his own wagon. Marta was on the seat, driving. Little Petey Mallory was riding with her, his thin body shapeless in the man-size cut-downs he wore, but grown up as hell in the gallantry of his attention to Marta and the opportunity to be man of the rig in Lavery's absence. The way Petey figured it, he and Cole Lavery were partners—honest-to-goodness partners in everything.

Marta was not wearing the gloves Lavery had bought her on the river. He looked at her hands. They were reddened and blistered where the heavy reins crossed the knuckles. Leaning forward in his saddle, Lavery touched one of them.

"You don't obey orders very well for a bride," he said.

Petey Mallory nodded. "She sure don't."

Marta laughed, then sobered. "The gloves, Cole? They'd wear out. Anyway, what kind of an emigrant's wife would I be if I showed up in Oregon or California with soft, tender hands? You're learning things, Cole. Let me learn, too."

Lavery nodded soberly. The country and the problems of assisting a train captain were not all he was learning. He was learning also about this girl he had married the day before he accepted this job with Captain Thoreson's wagon train. Thanks to the job, he and Marta would get to the Pacific Coast with a little profit to show for the crossing that cost most emigrants so much.

Since the night he had first seen Marta Strand, on the foredeck of a Missouri riverboat, she had become his greatest need. But he was just discovering that he did not really know her—that he didn't yet know the full strength of her character.

"You better pay off your help," he said. "We'll be pulling up shortly and Petey'll have chores at Ferris's fire."

The Mallory boy was sleeping nights under the Ferris wagon and riding days with Marta, while his two brothers were sick. Marta reached behind her and brought out a black japanned tin box with a peacock painted on it in bright colors. She unfastened the catch and lifted the lid. A music box concealed somewhere inside began to play the song of the wagon men: "Oh, Susannah!" Eyes bright, Petey reached over and picked out one of the clear, irregular amber crystals of the horehound candy it contained. Popping this into his mouth, he vaulted over the off wheel of the wagon, waved, and waited there in the dust for the Ferris rig to come up to him.

"We think this is an adventure for us," Marta murmured. "Think what it must be to a youngster, Cole. I wonder if that isn't why the wagons are rolling Westward, really . . . so kids can have all this emptiness and this room in which to grow?" Then, without waiting for an answer, her mood changed and she smiled. "How's the train tonight, Cole?"

"All right," Lavery said.

"You don't lie very well, Cole. Not to me. You'll want to report to Captain Thoreson. I'll be here when you come back. I always will be. Remember that. You were hired to do the worrying for the train and we're a partnership. You can't do your best if you're always thinking of me. Now, go on, but hurry back. . . ."

Lavery touched her hand again, smiled, and rode on. He could not help thinking of Marta, worrying about her as he worried about the train. They were deep into the Wyoming country. Too deep to turn back to Fort Laramie and too far from the Columbia tributaries to drop down to Fort Hall. The season was too far advanced for much more open travel. Somewhere in these friendless hills, winter was going to lock them in and they were going to have to halt with the crossing incomplete.

As if weather was not enough of a compulsion, Lavery was beginning to fear they had an ever greater threat facing them—this sickness of the Mallory kids and big Ed Kane and Captain Thoreson himself. It began to look like the scourge of wagon men. Among the Indians it was called the Black Death and frantically shunned. On the river it was known as the plague.

In a few days it would have moved from the presently affected wagons into others. No one in the train was safe from it; there would be no accounting afterwards for why some were stricken and others were not. It was the kind of gamble no man liked to face. And Marta was in one of the wagons.

Fitzhugh had come in from far ahead on the grass. The lean, grizzled scout was obviously troubled. He was riding a little distance from Thoreson's wagon, waiting for Lavery to come up. Cole reined in toward him.

"Well, Fitz?" he asked quietly.

The veteran trail man pulled off his fur cap and let the wind stir his long hair.

"Winter comes fast up here," he said. "Fast, hard, and

for keeps. That's storm weather up ahead. We've got till sunset tonight, the way I see it, to make up our minds whether we kill ourselves, trying to get on across, or whether we bed down sensibly till we've got decent spring traveling weather."

"There can't be much choice," Lavery said.

"How's the sick ones?" the scout asked.

"I think Kane's coming down. Know for sure what it is, Fitz?"

The scout brushed his fingers across his pox-pitted cheeks. "I ought to," he said dryly. "Look, Thoreson's too sick to think straight. That leaves you and me. Can you think of a way to get around the train articles and make these fools take our orders?"

"No. But wait here a couple of minutes, Fitz. I'll try once more to get Thoreson to back us up."

"I can tell you what he'll say before you ask him," Fitzhugh said sourly. "But go ahead. Try. And the rest have got such a fire on their tails to get where they're going that nothing I've said even dents 'em."

Lavery angled over to Thoreson's wagon and swung from his saddle to the box. A pot-bellied Kiowa, Thoreson's driver, made room for him. He wormed back under the hood. Thoreson's big frame was sprawled restlessly under the blankets of a bed in the wagon body. His huge leonine head was deeply sunk into its pillow. His eyes were half clouded, bright with fever. His breathing was rough.

"Fitz is back, Cap," Lavery said. "Snow's building on the range ahead of us. He doesn't think we ought to roll farther. We've got one wagon ready to break down. The stock isn't up to a hard pull. There's sign of more sickness today. We'd better winter."

"Your idea?" Thoreson asked.

"Mine and Fitzhugh's. We both think. . . ."

The man under the blankets stirred. His eyes fastened on Cole. "Let's get this straight, Lavery. I'm organizer and captain of this train. Fitzhugh was hired to guide us and to hunt. He's done a fair job, in spite of singing out wolf at every tough pull. You were hired to do the bookwork on wagons and stock and supplies and what saddle work along the string I didn't have time for. Neither you nor Fitzhugh was hired to think. You keep this string rolling, Lavery. I'm not going to be on my back long. . . ."

"I have been doing the inspection work, Cap," Lavery said. "That's why I'm telling you we can't go on."

"This is your first crossing, boy. We can't stop. Know what a train is made of? People. People stay in their own skins when they've got a chore for their hands every living hour they're awake. But give them idle time like there'd be in a winter camp and they climb right out of their skins. They start rubbing salt into others and letting others salt them. We've got good people and bad in our wagons, like there is in any train. I'm not going to give any of them a chance to show me what kind they are. I guaranteed every man who signed with me would see Oregon this year. I'm going to see they do it!"

"Alive or dead," Lavery breathed bitterly.

Surprisingly Thoreson nodded. "That's right. Bossing a train of wagons isn't a soft chore. You've got to do most of my work till I'm on my feet again. You've got to learn how the job has got to be done. The blood and the guts and the gravel, Lavery. Keep those wheels turning. Those are orders."

Lavery backed out from the hood and swung over into his saddle again. Fitzhugh rode up to him as he veered away from Thoreson's wagon.

"You were right, Fitz," he said heavily.

The old mountain man nodded grimly. "Cap isn't the first big man who thought he could be tougher than the mountains just because a lot of smaller folks were counting on him."

With uneasiness, Lavery pulled aside and waited for his own wagon to come up to him. He moved over to it, dropped his reins onto a rear body stake so his horse would trail, and stepped along a side rail to the box. Marta surrendered the reins of the team without protest when he reached for them. They jolted along in silence for a little time. Suddenly she leaned heavily against his shoulder.

"Cole," she said softly, "Cole, I'm afraid I don't feel very well. Not very well at all. . . ."

II

Captain Thoreson was in a heavy coma at nightfall. Fitzhugh did not like the bedding ground at which the string halted and he said so. It was in the open and a strong wind ruffled the wagon tilts, promising cold sleeping. There was a little valley south of the trail, well grassed and sheltered by a heavily timbered slope. Fitzhugh suggested this to Lavery, hinting that it would even make a good wintering place, but when Cole tried to swing the moving train off the broad Oregon track, there was immediate protest. The wagon train men were impatient. Like Thoreson, they did not want to lose several miles on a detour occasioned for mere comfort.

Fitzhugh disappeared. Lavery unspanned his personal animals, pegged them on close grass, and piled every piece of bedding between them onto Marta's bed. She protested.

"Feeling badly and being really sick are two different things, Cole," she said. "This is something I've got to get used to. With Captain Thoreson flat on his back, you've got more to look after than you can handle."

"I can handle you," Lavery told her with mock gruffness. "You stay here and don't move. I'll be back directly."

Swinging down from his own wagon, he went to look for Fitzhugh. The scout came out from behind a dark storage wagon. He was leading his horse, and his trail gear was lashed across the cantle of the saddle.

"There's only one way to work this, Cole," Fitzhugh said. "This outfit can't go on. It's up to us to stop them. You're just a greenhorn among them and they'll know you're bucking Thoreson's orders if you try to talk sense into them. It's different with me. I've passed word among them that I ain't going any farther West until the spring thaws come. I've told them I'll wait two days in that little bowl south of here. Then I'm heading East. It's up to you to make them believe I mean it."

"You think they'll be afraid to go on without a guide?"

"Listen, Cole," Fitzhugh said, "there's some damned fools in this train, but I doubt if the good God ever made an emigrant so wall-eyed crazy he'd head through this country without any idea of what he was getting into, and this is the first crossing for every man in this string but Thoreson and me. You won't have no trouble. They'll string their rigs into that little valley like sheep coming into a fold, soon as they've wore off their first mad at me." He swung up into his saddle. "Your missus was looking peaked this afternoon, Cole. How does she feel?"

"Not good, Fitz. But does that make any difference?"

"Not who's sick in the other wagons, maybe. But in yours, yes. To me, anyways. When a woman like her is sick, it's time she got every chance coming to her. Her kind is important to this country and has got to be taken care of."

The scout made a farewell gesture and rode back between the wagons toward the outer darkness of night. Lavery, head down and swearing at the bull-headedness of Thoreson and some of the others, strode toward the main fire of the encampment. But he doubted that Fitzhugh's device for halting the train would work.

Cosgrove and Mallory and Bill Ferris were crouched about the fire, the nucleus of a larger group ringing them. Beyond this knot of men the women were at work with food over the fire.

Big Ed Kane's wagon was closest to the fire. Kane, his face unnaturally flushed, and with a blanket drawn about his shoulders for extra warmth, was hunkered down on his wagon seat, looking at the group about the fire. Lavery heard a movement under the tilt at Kane's back and spoke to the big man.

"How is she, Ed?" he asked.

"It'll be tonight, she thinks. She ain't comfortable at all. Maybe she's been took already. Lavery, what do you know about borning kids?"

The man's concern was compelling. Lavery felt again his resentment at the other women of the train for their narrowness toward Ruth Kane. She at least had the whole-hearted concern and love of the man with whom she lived and this was more than some of the others could claim. He smiled at Kane.

"Enough to see your young one gets a fair start in this vale of tears, Ed," he lied with assurance. "I'll be handy when you need me."

Kane looked his gratitude and climbed back over the seat of his wagon. Cosgrove got up from his place by the fire and crossed to Cole, halting, spraddle-legged, before him.

"If you hadn't been so damned hasty over that cow, I could have splinted the critter up so she could have tagged with us, Lavery. She was my cow and you shot her, without my say-so. On the river you would have owed me something for that."

"We're a hell of a long way from the river, Cosgrove," Cole said sharply. "I've got a responsibility to every soul in this train . . . not to just you. We've been trying to make time. We couldn't afford delay for a cow."

Cosgrove swung on the others.

"That's what I mean!" he said. "I tell you, Lavery put Fitzhugh up to quitting us, figuring we couldn't get no farther without the old longhair. Lavery's a greenhorn. He kills my cow because he don't know better. We got no chance in his hands. I tell you, we got only one hope of getting across . . . and that's to tell Lavery to hell with him and what he says!"

Cosgrove's voice was inflammatory. Lavery saw cooler heads among the others, but he also saw determination. These men had moved their families from the places they had been rooted, promising a new country and a new home before winter. They were determined to keep their promises. Their stubbornness made them impervious to reasoning or counsel.

Mallory glanced uncomfortably at Lavery. "Two of my kids are sick and Petey's farmed out to Ferris and you. There's been talk of the plague. I hope to hell that ain't what it is, but I'm sure of this, Lavery. If we light for the winter at this altitude in country none of us knows, the plague is nothing to what's likely to happen to us. I say we should go on."

"It's cost us plenty to get this far," Ferris said. "I don't want to see that cost poured down a rat hole because a whiskery-faced old buckskin man and a young bucko with more nails than sense have both got a scare on."

"Train articles would let you elect a new temporary captain if you aren't satisfied with me, Ferris," Lavery said.

Cosgrove spat. "Why drag this out? What we're trying to tell you, Lavery, is that you're through. We've had us an election. The boys have hung it on me. As captain, I'm really going to roll this train. We've got the tracks of them ahead of us to follow. We don't need Fitzhugh. Starting tonight, we're making a quick sunset halt for chow and to rest the stock. Then we're rolling on another three hours in the dark before calling it a day. We're about ready to roll on now. You going to string with us, minding your own wagon, or do we leave you behind to make a winter camp with Fitzhugh?"

III

Cosgrove had the smugness of a man who believed in what he was doing, but who could not conceal satisfaction in his triumph over previous authority. Lavery was angry. Not at the smallness and smugness, but at the hardships that such a man's rocky judgment could work on others. Exhausted and sickening, these people and stock could not stand the strain of extra hours on the trail day after day. He lifted his head to answer Cosgrove, but at the same time a low outcry came from the interior of Kane's wagon. There was a stir at the ties and Kane thrust his head out.

"Lavery!" he called worriedly. "Lavery, it's started!"

"We've got to give Kane a hand now," Cole said to

Cosgrove. "I'll want one of the women. Some water heating on the fire, too. We'll talk tomorrow. Kane's wife and baby come first tonight."

Cosgrove shook his head. "Have I got to pound this between your ears, Lavery?" he demanded. "Our lives are mixed up in this. The risk's too great. We're moving!"

"But Missus Kane. . . ."

"There's some don't think she is Kane's missus, Lavery," Cosgrove answered callously. "Sure as hell, none of our women is going to climb into her wagon. Not at cost of keeping us all here. Ed can inspan and roll with us. His won't be the first baby born in a moving wagon along the trail. If his woman is worth her salt, she'll make out all right."

Others moved up behind their new captain, lending physical pressure to the stoniness of his refusal. Lavery's eyes were hard on Cosgrove's face. It was hard at Cosgrove's face that he struck. The blow snapped like a whip, and Cosgrove went down in the fireside dust, rolled slowly, and came up carefully with his hands raised to his injured face. Lavery could not tell if the man had stomach for more. Before Cosgrove picked up the issue, Petey Mallory ducked through the men and wheeled, crouched like a little dog, hackles up, beside Lavery.

In the same instant, Ed Kane's voice sounded raggedly from the seat of the wagon above them: "That's enough! Shin up here, Lavery. You and the kid, both. The rest of you get about the chores Cole ordered. One wrong move and I'll fire into the whole rotten-bellied lot of you!"

Lavery started up the spokes of the wagon wheel. Just over his head big Ed Kane rocked on the seat of his wagon, holding a smoothbore across his chest, its huge twin barrels covering the fire-lighted scene. Cosgrove and the others looked at the weapon in Kane's hands with respect. One or two of them, perhaps guilty of conscience, moved toward the fire as though to carry out Lavery's orders. For this instant the sick and outraged emigrant on the box was dominant.

Then, in the darkness beyond the wagon, there was movement. A thrown billet of firewood spun in, end over end. It struck Kane across the base of the neck, pitching him soundlessly forward across his own knees. His shotgun slid from his hands. Lavery stabbed for it, catching it by the barrel. A wagon man lunged in and wrenched it from him.

"Since you're so determined to give Kane a hand, and to hell with the rest of us," Cosgrove growled, "we'll leave you with him. The two wagons of you. Come up with us later, if you want to. But I'm warning you, you'll only have one more chance to make us trouble, Lavery!"

Petey Mallory, white-faced with anger, looked at Lavery. "Some of us stick together, anyhow, Cole," he said. "You and Ed and me. We got women to look after."

Mallory stepped out from the others and caught the boy's arm. "Missus Ferris is supposed to be looking after you, Pete . . . not Lavery. You get on over to her wagon right now."

"It's got to be that way . . . for now, Pete," Cole said.

"But I hired out to Missus Lavery. . . ."

Lavery remembered the little black japanned box then, the hours the boy had spent on the seat of the wagon beside Marta, talking in wonderment of the country through which they were traveling.

"She'll keep the job open, Pete," he said. "I'll tell her."

Tears were close to the surface in the boy's eyes, but he seemed to understand this was men's business, beyond his comprehension, and he backed away.

Another low outcry came from the Kane wagon. Lavery turned his back on Cosgrove and the others and started back up the wagon wheel. They broke then, beginning to scatter toward their own wagons. He climbed under Kane's tilt, side-stepping the inert form on the box. Ruth Kane looked up imploringly at him.

"Ed will be all right," Lavery told her. "Can you get by alone a few more minutes? I want to bring my wife down."

The woman smiled wanly. "I don't think any man realizes what a woman can put up with . . . when she has to. I'd like to have your wife with me, Mister Lavery, but I don't want to be a burden. You get Ed back on his feet. Then you go along with the other wagons. We'll do fine."

Lavery shook his head and stepped back out into the box. Kane was stirring. He sat up slowly. Lavery gripped his shoulder.

"You got some whiskey?"

Kane nodded assent.

"Take a good drink, then. Leave the bottle in the wagon where I can find it. Get your blankets out and make yourself a bed on the ground, out of the way. I don't like your color, Ed. You're too sick to be around this."

"You can't handle it alone."

"I'll bring down my wife. Before you roll up out of the way, see the fire's built up and some water is out where I can find it."

The big man nodded. Lavery went back up along the wagons, walking swiftly. Train men he passed ignored him as though completely absorbed in spanning in their own teams, but he caught covert glances and uneasy expression on some of the faces. He thought that the little group that had backed up Cosgrove at the fire was almost wholly responsible for the decision to replace Cole Lavery and to roll on westward. He thought that, if Cosgrove and Ferris and Mallory could be induced to reverse their stand, the rest of the train might agree to an immediate winter camp.

By the time he reached his own wagon, many of the others had already begun to roll. He saw Thoreson's wagon among them, the round-bellied Kiowa on the seat. He brought in his own animals. Marta heard him backing them over the tongue of the wagon and called to him.

"Cole, what's going on?"

"We're shifting camp a little bit. I'm going to move us back beside Kane's rig. His wife's starting to have her baby and Ed's too sick to do anything to help her. I'm going to call questions to you when I need help."

"I can do more than that, Cole."

"Not with the fever you're running," Lavery corrected gently. "We don't want Kane's baby to start life with exposure to the plague, do we?"

"I was afraid of that, Cole . . . the plague. You're sure?"

"I'm afraid so, girl," Lavery admitted raggedly.

"All right," she said. "I'm not afraid any more then. Not since I know. Ed Kane has it, too . . . and the others that are sick? Yes, take our wagon down beside Kane's. Ask me what to do. We'll make out."

By the time Lavery had worked his wagon down beside the Kane rig and pegged his animals out again, the rest of the train was rolling out of the camp. He watched it go with a mingled feeling of bitterness and concern.

Kane had followed his instructions to the letter. The fire was built up and a caldron of water hung over the flames on a folding iron tripod. The emigrant had already rolled into his blankets on the ground under the wagon, exhausted by even these small chores. Proof enough in itself of how sick Kane was becoming.

106

The details of the next few hours were hazy. Time passed without Lavery's awareness. What outcry Kane's woman made was driven from her. In the other wagon Marta talked calmly and soothingly—encouraging, listening to Cole's questions and answering them simply until it seemed his hands obeyed the impulses of her mind instead of his own. A little after midnight he climbed down from Kane's wagon and bent over the big man where he lay on the ground. Tiny sounds came from the wagon above.

"A boy, Ed. A fine one."

"And Ruth?"

"Tired, Ed. But all right."

The woman above heard the low-voiced exchange between them.

"A good, big boy, Ed!" she called. "This is the new beginning we've been waiting for. We don't have to wait till we've hit Oregon or California to start over. We've started now . . . tonight."

"Yes, Ruth," Kane said. He turned his head to Lavery. "I got to beg for something. Cole, could you look after the two of them for me? Just till I get this buzzing out of my head and this gripe out of my guts?"

Lavery nodded, but he was concerned. Things didn't get any easier. A sick man could not be put into a wagon with a new baby. A sick woman could not look after a new mother. And one man could not keep two wagons rolling. Yet it all had to be done.

He climbed under the hood of his own wagon and touched Marta's forehead. He could not tell who had the higher fever—Marta or Kane.

"Get Mister Kane in here with me, Cole," Marta said. "The ground out there is no place for a sick man. We can watch after each other and one of us can call if we need you. You'll have to stay with the other wagon, where you can watch over Missus Kane and the baby. Is it a cute baby, Cole?"

Lavery thought of the tiny, red, wrinkled face and grinned, but he nodded. Marta frowned.

"You didn't tell me the truth a while ago, Cole," she said. "The others have gone off and left us, haven't they? You're not commanding the train any more. What do we do, follow them?"

"No," Lavery said. "I can't risk taking you and the baby and Kane and his wife into the thing the rest of them are headed for. Fitz is waiting for us in his little valley south of here. We'll go there. I'll drive one wagon and tow the other. Fitz will be a good hand with you and Kane, Marta. He's had the plague and can treat it."

"What about you . . . and the others?" she asked. "You were hired to help Captain Thoreson look after them."

"Yes, I know. Still, they elected Cosgrove in my place. I don't know what I can do. . . ."

"You sure, Cole?" Marta insisted. "You sure you don't know what you want to do . . . what you've got to do?"

"Look," he answered with a faint flash of heat, "I've got my hands full, Marta . . . the Kanes, and you. . . ."

Marta smiled then, closing her eyes wearily. "I thought you'd be thinking of that. With Fitz on his feet, we'll be all right, Cole. I don't want you to leave, but if you have to. . . ."

IV

It was nearly noon when Fitzhugh rode out from a timber bosque above a beautiful little valley to intercept the two slowly moving wagons. Loss of sleep rode heavily on

Lavery. He was worn with the chore of swinging the double team hooked onto the first of the tandem-hitched wagons. Ruth Kane was resting with reasonable comfort in the wagon he was driving. The baby made the small occasional sounds of a satisfied infant. Marta and Kane were quiet in the following wagon. Cole greeted Fitzhugh with relief. The old scout took in the whole situation at a glance.

"Pulled out on you, eh?" he growled. "The damned, blind fools! Well, it's their hides. We'll be sound enough here, Cole. Got a place all picked out. Good water and plenty of game. Slopes sheltering snug. We'll put up a single cabin. We'll make it fair size and put all of us inside the one set of walls. Rub our natures a mite, maybe, but we'll be secure, with food and heat less of a problem when the weather really gets bad. Suit you, boy?"

Cole swung stiffly down from the wagon seat. "I haven't had time to think that far ahead, Fitz," he said.

Fitz cocked his head sharply, glaring. "You ain't thinking of being a damned fool, are you? You ain't thinking of shedding any more sweat over those idiots that pulled on out ahead?"

"I told you I hadn't done any thinking yet. I haven't slept since night before last. Trail your horse and climb up on that box, will you, Fitz? Roll these rigs on into the place you got picked out. We'll do our figuring after we've got both the teams outspanned."

Fitzhugh shrugged and climbed up onto the wagon. Cole made the reins of the mountain man's horse fast to a body stake and swung up into his own wagon. He poked his head through the lacing. Ed Kane seemed to be asleep. He was breathing heavily. Marta opened her eyes and looked up.

"How you making out, girl?" Cole asked. It was a kind of

silly question, but Marta didn't seem to think so. She smiled.

"Good," she said. "I'll bet I look better than you do and I'll take odds I feel near as good. You sure you're all right, Cole?"

Lavery nodded. "Sleepy, that's all. Now Fitz is with us, I can cure that."

"Sure," Marta agreed. "With Fitz here, there's no use worrying, Cole. Missus Kane and the baby are all right now. And Fitz will look after Ed and me. He'll have us on our feet in a hurry. You go ahead and take a good sleep. Take all you need. Please."

Lavery had worried steadily while he drove the lead wagon. It eased him to see Marta talking so clearly. It made his own inner struggle easier to know she had confidence in Fitzhugh. He started to back from the tilt.

Marta stopped him. "It's apt to be cold. Take your heavy jacket, Cole."

Lavery lifted the coat from its hook and draped it over his arm.

"Thanks, honey," he said. "I'll get my forty winks and then I'll see you."

Marta smiled again. "I think I'll sleep, too."

He pulled the lacings closed and dropped to the ground, walking along beside the wagon. As he did so, something banged against his thigh. Something in one of the deep pockets of the coat. He ran his hand into it, felt speculatively, then hurried forward, lifted the reins of Fitzhugh's horse from the body stake, and swung onto it. Reining it around, he rode up abreast of the box of the lead wagon.

"Your horse is better than mine," he said. "Mind if I use it, Fitz?"

Fitzhugh blinked.

"Better figure on just a temporary shelter, for now, Fitz," Lavery went on. "When I get back, we'll see how many cabins we have to build here."

"Back?" Fitz grunted, suddenly finding his voice. "Why, damn it, not even a green log like you is crazy enough to go after those others. They quit you. That's plenty. You've got your own troubles. Let's stick to them. Leave the others take care of theirs. The hell with them!" Fitz swung his head back and forth on his skinny neck in the heat of his anger. "I know what you think of your missus and I don't have to prod you about her, boy. But we both know she's worth more than the whole caboodle in the other bunch."

"I am thinking of Marta . . . of what she'd want me to do," Lavery said steadily. "I'll make it back as soon as I can. This is a job I tackled, handling this string. I got to do what I can."

"This is a hell of a country for a greenhorn saint to turn up in, Lavery," Fitz grumbled. "Sure, you can have the horse . . . anything I've got . . . but, man, why break your heart against a bunch like Cosgrove and his friends?"

"You'll take good care of Marta, Fitz?"

Fitzhugh leaned out of the wagon box and clamped a hand tightly onto Lavery's knee for a moment.

"We've got some mean and no-account gods in these high valleys and I'm not always on the best terms with the critters, but I'm going to talk mighty pretty to them all till you're back, boy. I'm going to do the best I can for your missus and the Kanes. You can figure on that."

Lavery nodded gratefully. "You won't have to say any-thing to Marta, Fitz. She knows. And it's all right."

Fitzhugh shrugged. Lavery reined away. Haste was im-portant. Cosgrove was leading the other wagons deeper into the hills each hour. Somewhere, not too far ahead of them, was a point beyond which none of them could be turned back.

He kept his back turned, not looking at the wagon where Marta lay. Instead, he pulled from his coat pocket the heavy object she had shoved into it. It was a little black japanned tin box. He opened the catch. Faint and tinny in the thin air, "O Susannah!" came out from somewhere inside of it, and the sun glinted on a little store of horehound crystals.

In late afternoon Lavery followed the wagons ahead onto a higher bench. The country was steeper, the loom of the mountains more pronounced. Heavy weather was swirling about their summits. Fitzhugh's horse was pretty well winded. The country was taking on an unreal air that Lavery decided was due to his sleeplessness. He hobbled the horse on the banks of a small creek and rolled out flat on the saddle blanket.

The chill of approaching evening roused him after a brief nap. Stiff and hungry, but somewhat refreshed, he saddled and rode on.

It was midnight when he caught a wink of fire ahead. He pulled up to survey the distant, carelessly circled hoods of the train.

He tethered his horse on a little patch of grass behind an aspen thicket some distance from the camp. With considerable care he reprimed his belt gun with French powder and recapped it. There seemed little other preparation he could make. Reaching into the pocket of his coat, he brought out the little japanned box, turning it over in his hand, but he did not open it.

Starting in toward the camp, Lavery stepped in the darkness into a freshly mounded patch of earth. With aversion he saw the rude cross heading it. A similar mound was a little distance away. There were two gone, then. Cole wondered who they were, but at the same time he realized that these two graves would be a powerful argument for the thing he wanted to urge. He thought maybe he could find listeners now.

There were half a dozen men hunkered down by the main fire in the encampment. Lamps glowed dully under the hoods of a few of the wagons. From somewhere in the camp came the outcries of someone in delirium. One wagon, dark, was rolled a considerable distance from the main group. Four others were scattered out along the perimeter of the camp. Lavery headed directly for the fire, cutting close to the nearest of the detached wagons.

He thought it deserted or its occupants all asleep, but when he was abreast of it, two shadows detached themselves from it, cautiously cutting out to meet him. Suddenly there was a small cry, heavily weighted with relief, and Petey Mallory flung himself at Lavery, only to pull up in a moment with an effort at maturity.

"Cole . . . Cole . . . !" The boy could go no farther. His voice broke.

Lavery recognized the other figure as the boy's father. Mallory spoke quietly: "I expected the devil here tonight, Lavery. Not you. I didn't think you'd be fool enough to follow us. Where's your wagon and Kane's? Everything all right in them?"

"Was when I left them."

"Where are they?"

"Where yours ought to be, Mallory," Lavery said bluntly. "Nearly a day down into the lower hills, where there's some protection against the weather building up. The place Fitz wanted us to winter in. He's there now, looking after Kane and his wife and their new boy and my wife. Look, Mallory, I just came across a pair of graves. . . ."

"Captain Thoreson's driver and my youngest," Mallory said quietly. "You trying to tell me you left your wife sick in the foothills and came on here to still try talking this bunch into turning back? Man, you're crazy! Look, don't try to get any closer than this to that fire over there."

"Why?"

"Well, the plague really hit us today, Lavery. A lot more wagons. Ferris's for one. That's why Petey moved back with us. Cosgrove figures he can stop the plague by turning iron-hard. Thoreson was alive when we made camp. Cosgrove tried to get his Indian to fall out of line and stay away from the rest of them with Cap's wagon, but the Kiowa kept on coming. Cosgrove shot him right off the box of the wagon. And him and the rest with clean wagons would give us out here on the edge the same thing if we moved in. Just a little while ago I heard more shooting. Your wife's sick. They know it. You're contaminated. They won't let you close."

This was utter folly. The disease was spread throughout the train. Attempts to segregate those infected and to partition the train should have been made days before. It was too late now. This was panic and it was dangerous. Those ill needed care.

"I'm going to have a talk with Cosgrove," Lavery said. Mallory seized his arm. "Man, I tell you you're crazy."

"You're forgetting that my wife and I weren't like most of you in the train, Mallory," he said quietly. "We didn't have any store of money and goods to speak of. Only our wagon. My job with Thoreson was paying our way . . . giving us a stake. If this train doesn't get on to Oregon, I can't collect my pay from the company. And if Marta and me ever see Oregon ourselves, we're going to need that stake."

Mallory grunted. This was something he understood.

"You coming with me?" Cole Lavery asked.

"I was ordered to stay out here," the wagon man said slowly. "They'll shoot me down like a damned dog. And my wife and the other youngster seem a little better. I got to stick with them . . . and with Petey."

The boy, a silent shadow between the two tall men, spoke up sharply: "Don't be figuring on me, Pa. I'm going with Cole."

Lavery reached in his pocket. "Oh, Susannah!" sounded. The boy reached forward.

"Pay in advance for this kind of work, Pete." Lavery said softly. "Marta sent it to you."

Mallory swore. He gripped the boy's shoulder and swung over beside Lavery.

"So she knew you were coming and sent you anyway," he breathed. "The kids in the string, eh? The women. And you talking about stakes and profits. The hell with you, Lavery. Seeing as at least two of the kids that are left are mine, I can walk any place you can, I reckon."

Lavery grinned and dropped a hand to the boy's other shoulder. The three started toward the big fire together.

V

Lavery knew Mallory had not been exaggerating when he had told of the panic and hysteria among the wagons. He knew this would be a tight squeeze. He wished he could have slept longer. His mouth was dry and his head hammering. Thirst was a suddenly mounting torment, of which he had been unaware half an hour before. Exhaustion, he supposed. A man could drive himself only so far, and then he began to come apart. Like this, he supposed. A funny, unsteady feeling in his legs. Distress in his belly. He brushed his hand across his eyes.

Mallory glanced quickly at him, but said nothing. A moment before those at the fire saw the three of them approaching, Lavery pulled his gun from his belt and eared the hammer back to full cock. He carried the weapon level, well out from his body in front of him, so that no man could miss seeing it. The hammering in his head seemed to increase with every step. The scene at the fire before him was unsteady. He saw Ferris rise up beside Cosgrove when a man at the fire spoke sharply. He glanced at Mallory.

"Think he should be segregated?" Mallory muttered. "Sure. But Cosgrove is on thin ice and needs him. Ferris quit his own wagon, left his wife in it, claims he's immune. Cosgrove's made the rest believe it. He's had to."

At the fire, Cosgrove sang out sharply: "That's far enough. Damn you, stay clear! Tom, who's that with you?"

"Cole Lavery, Cosgrove," Cole said. "You take it easy. I'm coming in . . . with my sights on your belly."

The men at the fire stiffened. Mallory fell in with Lavery, lagging a step behind. Only Petey kept abreast of the man with whom he walked.

Lavery struggled grimly to contain his own uncertainty. He did not know how to handle men such as Cosgrove—such as Ferris and the rest. He did not know their kind and he lacked Captain Thoreson's sure experience on the trail. He was, as Fitzhugh had told him, as much a greenhorn as any among them. But certain things were clear in his mind, remaining steadily in his consciousness in spite of the tired aching of his body and the hot, hammering turmoil in his skull.

The first was that duty was involved, a job unfinished.

The second was the thought of Marta, fighting for her life in their wagon in Fitzhugh's valley. The other half of the partnership they had sealed on the river. What he did was in part for her, since she had let him go—had given him freedom. Marta was a woman and there were women in this train. Women and kids.

"Stand quiet, Cosgrove," he said as the new wagon captain backed a step at the fire. "I'd rather kill two men than see twenty freeze in these hills. Don't make me prove it."

Cosgrove halted. Lavery came as close to the fire as was necessary and halted, also. Mallory was still a little behind him. Petey was at his side, big-eyed at being so deep in a man's affair, his small chin set like a rock, although the cheek above it bulged with a chunk of Marta's horehound crystal. Three yards away Cosgrove faced Lavery. Ferris was beside the new captain. There were three or four others in close to these two. The rest were farther back, undecided and uneasy.

"Thoreson tried to get out of his wagon tonight, Lavery," Cosgrove said. "He tried to argue we were fools to come so far with so many sick. He tried to keep us from shunting the sick wagons away from the rest of us. He tried to disarm me. Thoreson is dead, Lavery. He's the second one we had to kill. You get out of here. We're going on to the Coast in the morning. We'd as soon leave you dead as on your feet."

The chips were down then. The strain was tight against them all. The tenseness. And Cosgrove sure, with the others at his back. There was a gun in Lavery's hand and he could pull the trigger. He could kill Cosgrove. But he hadn't trailed these wagons to kill a man. He felt suddenly empty. He wanted a place where he could lie down. He wanted rest. And he knew he could not have it. Something had to be done—now—and he was the one who had to do it.

There was no sound for a moment. When the voice came, it did not belong to either Lavery or Cosgrove.

"You look funny, Mister Cosgrove," Petey Mallory said suddenly, with a youngster's acute observation, wholly disassociated from the tension of the moment. "You sure look funny . . . like Tommy, the day before yesterday."

Dully Lavery realized that the boy was referring to the first of his two brothers to take the plague—the one who now lay under freshly turned earth, out in the darkness beneath the aspens. And with that realization came another—that what made his head hammer, what made him unsteady and so raggedly on the edge of exhaustion was not strain and sleeplessness, but something else. He knew now that the dryness in his mouth was from fever, that he had been battling the first onset of the plague through the afternoon.

"Move away from the others, Cosgrove," he said. "That's your rule. You made it. And you're sick now, too. There's sweat on your hatband. There's hammers at work under it. There's a stink to your breath. . . ."

The hard brilliance of Cosgrove's eyes turned opaque. His lips straightened and flattened. He held onto himself, but the thought was at work in him.

"It won't work, Lavery," he said roughly. "Nobody'll believe you. I'm all right. I'm all right, I tell you . . . all right!"

"Nobody has to believe me. They can look at you. The boy saw it. I can see it. Ferris is standing beside you. He can see it. Look, he's backing away! It's there. The flush. Backache. Is that a pox there under your collar already? Have you kept how you were feeling quiet that long? Get away from him, all of you. Get away!"

It was like watching a rope on which too great a strain

has been placed. Fiber after fiber snapping with little soundless bursts of frayed hemp, each one following the preceding one a little more quickly, until in a handful of minutes there was only the core. And this going. . . .

Cosgrove launched himself forward, shouting: "Shut up, you fool! Shut up!"

VI

Lavery tried to twist away from the rush, but his own unsteadiness, the agony in his skull and his body, which had hammered at him mercilessly for hours, betrayed him now. He lost his footing and went clumsily to one knee. Utter savagery was in Cosgrove's face. Cole did not know if the man was fevered with the plague or not. He could not tell if the savagery was only the desperation of a man who was afraid of an idea instead of a fact. He knew only that he had recounted his own feelings and that, if the man was sick, they had struck home. He saw Cosgrove swing one heavily booted foot. Only then did his own slowed reflexes function. His gun fired. He tilted on over, realizing that he had fallen onto his face, but not knowing whether this was an inward collapse or something into which he had been driven by Cosgrove's swinging boot.

His belly was wrapped in something that was not so much pain or sickness as a desire to find quiet and motionlessness and coolness. A desire built in his body and apart from his mind, to escape the disease with which it struggled. He wanted consciousness to leave him. He wanted escape. He had failed here. He had made a play and fired a shot and he had fallen on his face. Now he wanted to forget, to rest, to sleep.

119

But he could not shake all impressions. Turmoil. People shouting. Mallory and Petey bending over him. Increasing coldness in the wind. The *creak* of wheels and the jolt of obstacles under them, slamming up through stout oak and hickory to shake his sick, struggling body.

Once he thought that he sat upright, swearing with all of the sulphur and bitterness that had accumulated since Captain Thoreson fell sick, at the men who had tried to bull through the hills. He thought he charged men with Thoreson's death, with the Kiowa's death, with the death of Mallory's oldest boy, and promised the judgment of savage gods on every man in the train if Marta was not better when he returned to her. He thought it snowed, hard, on a rising wind. But he did not know if any of these things were true.

The first day that Lavery could shave, Marta seated him in a pole chair by the open window, from which the rawhide screen had been removed. Bright sunlight came in from the snow-covered meadow, and a wind softer than any he had known in an Eastern winter. Smoke arose from the stone stacks of the other cabins making a little square on the edge of the meadow. Paths were shoveled clean from one to another. Petey Mallory and his older brother and three or four other kids were building a huge snowman on the edge of a drift piled against the back of the communal stock shed.

Marta brought Cole his stropped razor and a pan of steaming water and a dish of soap. She left the mirror turned face down across his lap for a moment.

Marta looked as fresh as the snow outside. Old Fitz had understood the plague and its treatment and Marta had owned the courage. Ferris, immune, had tried to escape the valley camp after the return of the wagons, still fearing he would take the disease. It had been three weeks before they found him in the snow. There had been little to bury. Cosgrove was also planted shallowly in the meadow sod, waiting for spring thaws for a deeper grave. He had made himself too hard. His metal would not stand the tempering to which he subjected it. He had been brittle and he had broken. Fitz had said he would survive the pox. But he had been too afraid of the disease, and his fear would not let him mend.

Sitting in the sunlight of the window, Lavery thought of these things. Fitz had known how to treat the plague, all right, for those who had fight in them. Kane had recovered. And Marta was unmarked. He was happy about that. He had not wanted her altered. He smiled at her and she lifted his shaving mirror, holding it from him a moment longer.

"You're changed a little, Cole," she said quietly. "I wanted to tell you first. You were on your feet too long after the fever came. The pox was already broken out on you when you reached here. There wasn't much Fitz could do then. The pox left scars. Believe me, Cole, these scars of yours are like the lines of a face . . . they mean something. Living, for one thing . . . sacrifice. . . ."

Marta broke off. Cole understood what she was trying to tell him. He lifted the mirror. A face he didn't know looked at him. Not an unpleasant face. The scars were not ugly. The smoothness of his cheeks was roughened, but the pox had done more than that. It had highlighted the planes and angles of his features. Even to his own eyes, a quiet sureness and strength was evident, as though the plague had stripped away a mask to reveal what had always been underneath. He reached for his shaving soap. Marta smiled then, and went to the window.

"Ruth Kane and Betty Mallory and I have been inquiring," she said. "The others will surrender any claim they might have to the buildings here when they leave in the spring. And they're willing to trade a lot of supplies and equipment for our big wagons. The trail is going to see a lot of travel, Cole. And this is our first home. I'd like to stay. The Kanes and the Mallorys and us. We could make a way station here and sell supplies to passing wagons . . . raise some of the stuff ourselves. It would be a good thing, for a while, anyway. And Oregon will always be on West, when we want it. Would it be all right, Cole?"

This was the kind of partner of which a man dreamed—a partner with her eyes open. A man or woman was a fool who believed the crossing to California or Oregon was for gold or timber or land alone. In the end, Lavery thought, the folks in every train were not so much after gold or land as after freedom and room to build something of their own making.

He reached up for Marta and she bent toward him, then laughed and twisted down onto his lap. Through the screen of her hair, Cole saw the faces of Petey Mallory and his brother appear at the open window. Petey shoved his brother roughly and the two disappeared.

Petey's voice came in the window: "We can come back later, Ted. That's important business in there!"

Petey was right. It was important. Important as hell.

Lavery's shaving mug slipped from the arm of the chair and rolled unheeded to the floor.

Trail of Whitened Skulls

The author titled the fourth Cole Lavery story "Satan Cursed a Wagon Train" when he sent it to his agent on April 26, 1948. Because Rogers Terrill had bought his first wagon train story with Cole and Marta Lavery and changed their names, in order to continue the Cole Lavery saga in pulp magazines Blackburn felt he had to write another wagon train story using these characters by name. In the first wagon train story, the couple had been heading to Oregon. In this story, they are heading to California. Mike Tilden at Popular Publications bought the story for *New Western* but this time paid the author only .022¢ a word. That came to $198. Tilden altered the title to "Trail of Whitened Skulls" when it appeared in *New Western* (9/48). For its appearance here the magazine title has been retained.

I

Cole Lavery had for several days been conscious of a peculiar feeling of nostalgia he could not define. Certainly there was nothing familiar to him in this arid, blistered country. Farther back toward the river, yes. There he had seen plots of virgin ground and wooded slopes that needed only a little closing of the eyes to take on the appearance of the lush

123

Kentucky valleys where he had been born. He was washing in a basin beside the wagon, noting that the fine gleaming varnish of the stout Murphy was already badly cooked and peeling, and considering the problem that lay before every wagon owner in the train—the course the outfit should follow the rest of the distance to California.

Marta came out from under the tilt and climbed down the wheel to stand beside him. The crossing had agreed with Marta better than it had with the Murphy wagon. He had thought she was beautiful when he had first seen her in the forepeak of a Missouri riverboat, beating up to Westport. She had seemed the embodiment of the freshness and challenge of the new country when she stood before a minister in the river town the night before the train rolled, solemnly agreeing to accept a share in whatever he found beyond the mountains. The heat and the dust and the interminable monotony of the crossing had brightened these virtues in her. She smiled at him, and then, turning her face into the wind, she identified the source of the nostalgia that had been puzzling him.

"I never saw so much dust," she said. "But it doesn't seem to be in the air. Funny, isn't it? The air's almost cool, even when the sun is so hot. And a kind of a fresh smell. Almost like the ocean."

That was it. The ocean. Lavery remembered two summers on the Atlantic when he was a boy. It was this he was remembering. And the freshness did come from an ocean. The strangest ocean in the world.

"McIntyre says we aren't over forty miles north of the Great Salt Lake," he said. "The wind is south. Maybe that's where the smell comes from."

"The Salt Lake," Marta said. "Too bad we won't see it. I'd like to."

"You will," Lavery told her quietly.

Marta's thick brows raised. "But Cole, I thought you said the train just couldn't turn south here, that this short cut Bert McIntyre has been trying to sell the others on was too dangerous. Didn't you argue it last night at the owners' meeting?"

"McIntyre argued better than I did," Lavery said wearily. "He had persuasion I couldn't use. In the first place, he's been to California twice before."

"Not over this short cut of his," Marta put in.

"No," Lavery agreed. "But he's a veteran of the crossing and more likely to get listeners than a greenhorn like me. And he's promising to save two weeks of travel. What does safety amount to against time saved in the rush to the Sacramento gold creeks? I was kicked off the council last night, Marta."

Lavery had been debating how to break this news. Marta was young enough to take satisfaction in her husband's accomplishments. She relished being the wife of a wagon train councilman. He thought this would be a blow to her, but he had forgotten Marta's practicality.

"Then we'll do what we feel is right and let the rest of them go to . . . well, to wherever they're going," she said.

Lavery shook his head. "We aren't leaving the train."

"Then you believe McIntyre is right . . . that this southern short cut of his is practical?"

"I think that, if this train swings very far south on the track McIntyre urged, the chances are a lot of wagons won't see California," Cole told her softly. "That's why we've got to stick with them."

"Look here, Cole," Marta said with mock severity, "there's a few like you west of the mountains, greenhorn or no. But you've got only two hands and there's a limit to what you can do. You can't turn thirty stubborn men out of a track they want to follow. Bert McIntyre doesn't like you.

He'll make you sweat every foot of the way."

"When a man can't use his hands," Lavery said grimly, "he has to use something else."

"What do you get out of it? What makes us richer by going with them than by waiting here for another train along the northern road?"

"Nothing," Lavery admitted.

Marta grinned at him then, dropping her severity. "Then this half of our partnership votes with you," she said. "I can't stand a man who'd make a fool of himself for a profit, but I reckon I could tolerate one who makes a fool of himself because he figures he's right."

Marta leaned over and brushed her lips against his. Lavery pulled on his shirt and started up the bent line of wagons toward the wire-braced Conestoga belonging to Bert McIntyre.

McIntyre was a big and raw-boned man of the kind bred up from the soil. A man who owned no pleasant memories and whose sole interest and hope lay in what was ahead, not in what he had already known. Approaching the man where he leaned against the tailboard of his wagon, at breakfast on his feet, Lavery did not think McIntyre was the fearless kind a man occasionally encountered. There were things Mac wanted and things he didn't want. There were men he liked and men he didn't like. Lavery doubted his thinking went beyond this.

"You choused me away from the fire last night before I had a chance to find out when we were rolling. Since we're heading toward what might be a dry crossing, I suppose we'll take a couple of days, fitting out here, before we turn south."

McIntyre looked him over slowly, chewing at the food in his mouth with an animal thoroughness. He swallowed before shaking his head.

"Glad you came up here, Lavery," the gaunt farmer said. "You an' me have gotta know how we stand. The boss wheel in this outfit is going to have only one spoke from here on, and I'm it. That suit you?"

"Why not?" Lavery countered. "I've got no cause for complaint, yet. Time enough to say so when I do have . . . if ever."

"That's the point," Bert McIntyre growled. "Complaints is filed now or not at all. Them that are dissatisfied here can say their piece and split off from the rest of us now. Once wheels start turning again, there's going to be no more trouble. Country to the south ain't exactly gentle. We can make it easy if we watch our water and cross fast. But if some of us ain't pulling with the rest, the whole lot will bog down. I could be pretty rough on a troublesome man if I thought he was risking the rest of the outfit. Make myself clear?"

Lavery nodded. "I got to be understood, too," he said steadily. "I'm sticking with the train. Not because I think you'll get me to California any quicker than I'd make it if I held on across the northern route. I'm not even sure I'll ever see California with you. But I've got friends in this train and my wife has friends. I think you're apt to kill some of them. But I won't make you trouble. You've got my word. I get a chance to vote, I'll vote with the majority. That's a promise. If there's no voting, I'll keep my jaw shut."

McIntyre spat carefully. "All right," he said.

Lavery saw the satisfaction growing in the man. Obviously the farmer thought Lavery was crawling a little. This was a mistake. McIntyre should know, as Marta had instinctively known, that a man like Lavery did not reverse a bet unless he had seen another way to play out a hand of cards.

"You've been to the coast before," Lavery said curiously. "What's your hurry to get across the desert and the Sierra, this time?"

The gaunt man spat again. "It takes money to buy the kind of land I want out there. I know better than to sweat over the gold. I'm a land man and it's land I want. I've made a little money taking California riding stock to the East. I'm making a little money guiding this train West. I'd sure make more if I could get more trains to guide. Think of the business I could do if I took this one across to the Coast two or three weeks ahead of the best time schedule possible on the Donner track for instance? If I could do that, I could have me a name. A couple of more seasons and I could buy the damnedest *rancho* in the Californias."

"You'd risk thirty wagons and the lives of the folks riding in them to build yourself a reputation?" Lavery protested.

McIntyre whittled himself a twig of greasewood with half a dozen strokes of his knife and began to pick his teeth with the splinter. He smiled slowly.

"I got no kin in this string," he said. "A man gets along by hauling on his own bootstraps. The rest in this outfit are in a hell-fired hurry. I told them the truth about what I knew of this cut-off and they voted to take it. . . ." The man paused and ran his thumb along the keen edge of the knife. "Mind your own wagon, Lavery," he added.

Cole nodded. "I sure as hell will, Mac," he agreed.

II

Four days below the branching of the cut-off, two days after the wide, glaring sands of the salt fields north and west of the Great Salt Lake had been skirted, the last of the bunch grass faded out, reducing forage to a stringy, sparse kind of saw grass. The coat sheen of the train animals began to roughen a little and ribs showed here and there.

Bert McIntyre kept them on water at night, but it was poor water—the worst they had seen in the long crossing. Several of the children were down with the grippe and a man instinctively avoided drinking more than a minimum amount in spite of a chronic thirst bred of the brassy heat of the day and the extreme aridity of the wind.

The sink at which McIntyre bunched the wagons at the fourth night stop lay at the base of a black butte of raggedly eroded lava, flanked by low, sloping ridge folds of twisted limestone and granite.

Marta stood beside Lavery, watching as he blew a small, intensely hot supper fire of greasewood to proper heat for her.

"I'm afraid, Cole," she said. "The grass isn't good. The water gets worse . . . and the heat. And the country . . . Cole, I think this must be the place where the world was born." She nodded toward the tortured folds of the hills. "Agony made those ridges. Birth pains, Cole. And there's still hurt out here. Hurt for all of us. I wish we hadn't turned south with the others."

"We're still traveling," Lavery said. "We're still camping on water. And we're four days closer to California."

Marta looked evenly at him. "It's all right to lie to McIntyre and the rest, Cole. But it doesn't go with me. You're not meek or mild, and I'm worried about what's going on in your mind. You're planning something for Bert McIntyre. I'm afraid it'll lead you into trouble."

Lavery stood up. He wanted to tell Marta what he was thinking. But his plan sounded a little silly in his own ears, and its one hope of success lay in keeping it wholly to himself. He planned to work on the minds of everyone in the train. He could not do this if any of them knew what he intended. Even Marta. He shook his head.

"Nothing will happen to Mac that he hasn't asked for," he said.

Marta shrugged. "Missus Wilson had me look in on her little girl. The youngster's pretty sick. Missus Wilson hoped I'd know what it was. I didn't. Missus Wilson is worried. So am I, Cole."

"Kids don't have the iron that grown-ups do," Lavery said casually. "This is bad water. Yesterday's was bad, too. Might be some kind of poison in it. Maybe the same thing that's been causing the grippe in the other youngsters."

Marta looked serious. Lavery gave his attention again to the fire. Marta moved off after a little. Presently he saw her talking to Clem Wilson's wife beside their wagon.

Marta came back to the fire. In a way, this was using pretty dirty cards. But at their worst, they were not as bad as the personal ambition that was driving Bert McIntyre.

Marta brought out the skillet and her pots and rigged them by the fire. Lavery went for water with a little oaken bucket. Forsythe was at the edge of the black-rimmed sink, filling a canvas container. He eyed Lavery uncertainly, brushing impatiently at the soft brim of his hat, blown down across his eyes by the fitful, gusty pressure of the wind.

"I could do with a gale or a calm. This in-between chafes hell out of me," Forsythe said.

"It'll get worse before it gets better," Lavery told him.

"How's that?" Forsythe asked sharply.

Lavery shrugged. "Seems I heard it," he said carelessly. "Something about the wind down this way. Only time it doesn't blow is midwinter. Take the tilt off a wagon if it isn't netted down with a lot of lines laced over the outside."

"That's a hell of a lot of wind," Forsythe said.

"This isn't what I'd call a breeze," Lavery answered, turning his back to a heavy gust coming across the sink.

130

Forsythe filled his canvas container with a sudden, impatient dip and strode back toward his wagon. Lavery grinned at the stiffness in Forsythe's departing back.

Marta and Cole were lazing on a tarp beside the embers of the fire, their dinner warm in them. McIntyre approached, removing his hat in deference to Marta. Lavery noted this and again considered the girl he had married. She was quiet and it took time to realize the forcefulness of her nature. This was the first time Lavery had seen Bert McIntyre uncover before any woman in the train.

"Excuse me, Missus Lavery," McIntyre said sullenly, "but Clem Wilson has been raising hell, over to my wagon. His missus has been talking to you, I gather. Something about poison in the water we been drinking. What kind of poison is it?"

Marta looked up in surprise, shot a quick glance at Cole, and rose to her feet.

"I was making a guess, Mister McIntyre," she said. "How do I know what kind of poison it is? All I know is that half the youngsters in the train here got the grippe, and that the little Wilson girl is right sick. You know this country and this trail. You tell me what it is."

Lavery drew a slow, deep breath of satisfaction.

McIntyre colored deeply. He pulled his hat back onto his head. "Talk," he snorted. "I tell you, there's got to be a stop to it. Why, hell . . . excuse me, ma'am . . . I'll have the ringiest set of fools in the country on my hands if something like that really gets a start."

"Then you better halt us nights by better water than we've been getting the last couple of days," Marta said bluntly.

The wagon boss backed a little way from the fire, making a summoning gesture of his head to Lavery. Cole rose and followed the man into the night.

"Forsythe is talking about wind to the south. Bad wind. Got it from you. Where'd you hear of it?"

"I don't remember," Lavery answered easily. "In a camp somewhere. Bear River, maybe. Or the Laramie Fork."

"Whereabouts do we hit this wind?" McIntyre demanded.

Lavery matched Marta's shrug. "Never been this way, myself. High wind in a dry country like this, with water scarce as hell, would play the devil with stock and tempers both, now, wouldn't it?"

McIntyre glared at him, turned, and stalked away. Lavery glanced back at his own fire. Marta was busy with the pots and dishes there. She would not miss him for a little. He stepped away from the wagons, moved obliquely toward the outer darkness where one man stood on guard over the stock.

The stock, on hobbles, was restless. Poor forage, short water rations, and the steady, driving pace McIntyre had been maintaining with the string had combined to make them so. Their movement concealed Lavery's approach.

The guard was Ed Simon, Bert McIntyre's nephew—a pimply, overgrown youngster who had grown arrogant since the emergence of his uncle as captain of the wagons. He was keeping an indifferent watch.

Lavery came easily up behind him, set himself, and called out softly in a formless word—something that might sound to a startled man like a shout. At the same time, he struck with his balled fist, aiming at the union of Simon's neck and shoulders. The boy half turned at the sound, with a premonition of alarm. His mouth fell open and continued to hang loosely as the shock of Lavery's blow slackened nerves. But his big body gave Lavery trouble. His turn had partially deflected the force of the impact, and he did not go

132

down but remained on his feet, rocking stupidly and uncertainly back and forth.

Impatiently Lavery cut another blow at him, this time connecting with the flat plane of his jaw line. Simon buckled, then, and pitched forward onto his face.

Moving hurriedly, Lavery cut through the stock, slipping the hobbles on those of the extra animals he judged would be of least value to the company. The freed stock moved aimlessly for a moment. Then realization of freedom seemed to strike them and they drifted off through the night, bunching together and picking up speed.

Lavery grinned wryly. It struck him as a paradox of sorts that draft animals, admittedly short on intelligence, could recognize an error in judgment so readily and so easily find a remedy for it—the old one of putting one foot ahead of the other in the right direction—while their masters bought the bad advice of a man like McIntyre.

When he had freed a dozen animals, Lavery cut back toward the camp, entered it between the Wilson wagon and his own, and approached his fire as though returning from the most ordinary of errands. Marta was hanging her dishcloths, freshly laundered after their evening service, on a line stretched across the tailgate of the wagon.

She eyed Cole with what he thought might be speculation, but she said nothing. He yawned. She smiled at him, then, and preceded him into the wagon.

III

The alarm came twenty minutes after Lavery turned in. Marta, who had filled the day with activity and who had not been waiting for something, had gone immediately to sleep.

She aroused at the first sound—Ed Simon's high, nasal voice, spilling out an incoherent jumble.

When Lavery leaped down to the ground and started on a trot toward McIntyre's wagon, where the others were gathering, Marta came with him, pulling a wrapper closely about her.

There was a blue swelling discoloring Ed Simon's jaw and fear was big in his eyes. His uncle, short of temper, caught his shoulder and shook him savagely.

"Quit howling!" McIntyre snapped. "What the hell happened out there?"

"The stock," Simon bubbled. "Indians!"

"I asked you what happened, damn you!" McIntyre growled. He wiped his open hand smartly across Simon's face. "Talk it straight!"

"If there's stock lost, we better look for it instead of listening to talk," Lavery suggested.

"When I want something out of you, I'll ask for it," McIntyre snapped. But the seed was planted. Two or three of the others, notably Forsythe and Clem Wilson, nodded agreement and started to move out toward the hobbled animals. McIntyre barked an order at them.

"We'll go when I give the word. Something is crazy as hell. There ain't any Indians in here. Couldn't be. And if there was, you two would be as stupid as this young fool here to go out there into the night alone. Stand in your tracks till I can make sense out of this."

He turned back to his nephew. Simon wiped a reddened hand across his bloody lips and glowered angrily at his uncle, but he talked more coherently.

"I was trying to do my job right," he said. "Not standing still, looking at the stars, like some of the others I've seen on guard. I was circling the stock. I seen these shadows.

Knew right off what they were. Thought I could double in
past them and maybe turn the camp out so's we could catch
them red-handed."

McIntyre nodded impatient approval.

"They must have been in two parties. Stumbled right into
the second one while I was watching the first. Big devils,
painted to hell. Hatchets in their hands. One made a pass at
me. I fed him a fist and busted loose. But the rest landed on
me. Got me off my feet and used their boots on me."

"Boots?" Lavery cut in mildly. "On Indians?"

"He means moccasins," McIntyre snapped. "Damn you,
Lavery, keep your trap shut."

"Got me in the middle of the neck, then, in the face,"
Simon went on with a sullen look at Lavery. "That's all I
remember till I came around and found the stock gone."

"All of it?" Forsythe asked.

"I don't know," the boy said.

"We better find out," Forsythe said.

Scowling, Bert McIntyre nodded. He shoved his nephew
away from him with an impatient violence that staggered
the youth. "If I find you been lyin' . . . if sign says you was
asleep out there . . . !"

He left his promise of violence unspoken, but his intent
was unmistakable. Forsythe and Wilson and several others,
rifles slung across in front of them and ready, moved away
from the wagons.

Talk, the flaring of matches for light occasionally, and
the sound of considerable movement drifted back in among
the wagons. Presently the party returned. A baffled look
was in Bert McIntyre's eyes. The others looked a little
puzzled, but genuinely alarmed.

"About a dozen head gone. The worst of the lot, generally
speaking," Wilson told the gathered company. "No sign of

Indians, now at least. Simon wasn't keeping the best watch in the world. Where he'd been hunkered all evening was plain enough, and that was where he fell. But something roughed him and something made off with the stock . . . slipping the hobbles on those they wanted, leaving the rest be."

"Had to be Indians," Forsythe added. "Coyotes are smart in this country, but not that smart, and there ain't nothing else big enough. Mac, we into Indian country yet? You said it was still some piece ahead."

"Maybe we could have got to the edge of it," McIntyre muttered.

Forsythe nodded. "I figured that. Kind of accounts for this. Bound to be damned poor and ornery Indians in such a damned poor and ornery country. Way I see it, they only took what they thought they could get away with. And they right carefully didn't cripple us, figuring that, if we didn't get pushed too hard now, we'd keep on moving . . . right in to where they could really work us over."

"That's no way to talk," McIntyre protested uneasily.

"It sure as hell ain't," Forsythe agreed with rising dissatisfaction. "I tell you, Bert, you been doing most of the talking the last week. Supposing you try it, now. See if you can make your talk sound any better."

McIntyre eyed the circle of those surrounding him. Lavery saw with satisfaction that a number of them had begun again to do their own thinking—that the bright chimera of an early arrival on the California coast did not appear as attractive to them as it had the night they had elected McIntyre captain and guide.

The wagon boss finally spoke sullenly. "An outfit has got to pull together," he said. "All together. Like a ship at sea. Get somebody pulling the wrong way and it jinxes the whole shebang. We got kids sick, and now Indians snatch some stock. It's more'n bad luck. It's a jinx."

He was looking at Lavery. One or two of the others turned and looked in the same direction. Forsythe broke it up.

"Maybe," he said. "But we got to do something. We going after that stock, or aren't we?"

"We better," McIntyre decided. "Take ten men, Forsythe. Ten men with rifles and good horses between their knees. See what you can do. They can't have gone far."

"Not me, Bert," Forsythe said. "I'm not getting that far from water. I don't know this country. You're the guide. You asked for the chore. If you can get ten of the boys to ride with you after a dozen head of stock we can do without, go ahead. Me, I'm going back to bed."

"You disobeying orders?" McIntyre asked raggedly.

"Figure that out for yourself," Forsythe said angrily. He stalked off toward his own wagon. Marta caught Cole's arm and pulled insistently at it. Lavery turned with her and they started back toward their own tilt. When they were out of earshot of the others, Marta stopped, arms akimbo, and glared at him.

"All right, Chief Horse Thief," she said. "You weren't gone twenty minutes after supper. I don't know how you freed all those animals in that time. But if I'm going to live with an Indian, I think he'd better tell me just whose side he's on."

Lavery rounded his eyes. "Squaw talk too much," he said noncommittally. "Me sleepy."

And he climbed back into the wagon, saving the grin of elation with which he had been struggling until the darkness under the tilt masked it.

Marta had apparently been doing some thinking during the night. At breakfast she was silent half through the meal.

Ed Simon came down along the line of wagons on some errand, and, despite the pot of good-smelling coffee on Marta's fire and Lavery's good morning nod, the boy circled wide of them.

A moment or two later, Mrs. Wilson came out behind the neighboring wagon to string up a little wash so that the drippings, at least, would be out of it before the train rolled. Marta spoke to her. The woman heard the greeting, but she did not turn her head. Presently she went on back to the front of her wagon.

"Cole," Marta said quietly, "we've got Lutherans and Baptists and Methodists and Catholics in this train of wagons. All good people. Reasonable enough, all of them, and some of them well-educated. But what you're doing is dangerous. There's something about this country . . . something about this few of us being alone together out here in all this endlessness and wildness . . . which seems to make reasonableness a scant thing. Like the country itself was turning the years back on us all . . . sending us a long way back toward the time when we were all pagans. Have you noticed how much superstition has been talked about since we left the river? Have you noticed how jumpy some of these people have gotten, how ready to believe the most ridiculous tales we've heard along the trail?"

"Sure," Lavery agreed. "What's it mean? Why dangerous to me? I'm convinced McIntyre's leading this outfit into a terrible experience. I can't very well stand up against every man in this train. I've got to do the next best thing . . . sort of cut the ground Mac is standing on out from under him. And without hurting the others too much. Sort of a business of having to be cruel to be kind."

"Nobody is going to realize that you actually turned those horses loose last night. Nobody is going to realize you actually do any of the other things you've probably got in mind. You're too careful for that. But there was talk about jinx, Cole. Jinx is something nobody understands. And people who are troubled are more afraid of something they don't understand than anything else. If they get to thinking that you're a jinx . . . that we are . . . it can mean real trouble for us."

Lavery grinned. "You're too sharp," he complained. "It's a good thing the rest of the people in this string of wagons aren't onto me like my wife is, or my plan wouldn't work. Look, Marta, I don't care who they think is the haunt that is bringing them bad luck. What's important is that they all get to thinking they've had bad luck since they turned south. If I can make that happen soon enough, the whole string will turn back to the northern route . . . and that's what I want."

Marta nodded. "I know. I don't want to see women like Missus Wilson have any more hardship. I don't want to see the children have any more. I'd like to see the men in the string arrive in California on their feet and strong, so that they can take hold in the new country and root down quickly. I think that's worth some risk to you, and to me. Like you, I don't see any other way the two of us can turn the wagons back. I promised you on the river we'd be partners. We're partners in this and you should have let me in on it in the beginning. But there's only one thing. . . ."

Lavery could see that Marta was gravely troubled. He had been over this in his mind a dozen times, and he believed he had countered every flaw in his scheme. If it worked, it would work well. If it failed, the only result possible was estrangement from the rest of the people in the train for Marta and himself. And California was so close that this could easily be borne. He smiled reassuringly.

"Pour me another cup of coffee and let's hear what you're worrying about. It's nearly time to inspan the teams and start rolling."

"Supposing everybody does get to feeling we're a jinx? If nothing very serious happens . . . nothing worse than losing a few head of stock and maybe a little annoying wagon breakdown here and there, all right. I know you. You wouldn't attempt anything else. You'd be afraid of hurting somebody. The train people would growl about us, and, if they were hampered enough, they'd turn back, still growling. The growls wouldn't hurt us. But you've been afraid this is bad country McIntyre is leading us into . . . that the train faces terrible things. Supposing everybody is more stubborn than you think and they don't turn back soon enough? Supposing one of the terrible things you've been afraid of does happen . . . while we're with them and while everybody believes Cole Lavery is a jinx? That's what I've been thinking about."

Lavery frowned. This was something he had not considered. Marta was right—superstition seemed to hang like a cloud over the people on the move. Few of them seemed content to think as individuals—they just followed the lead. If life and death became involved in the bad luck facing the train, then these people would think in terms of life and death in retaliation. It could be dangerous—even more dangerous than perhaps Marta realized.

Marta was watching him closely, uneasiness in her eyes. Lavery straightened. He wanted the wagon train men troubled. And he was troubled himself, now. But he wanted Marta to carry no worry. He answered her with a grin.

"The train isn't going to get far enough south to have more trouble than it's already had, girl," he said easily. "Laverys have been jinxes for generations. When a Lavery

140

puts his mind to it, he plain breathes a hex into the air and nothing can go right for anybody around him. Now, if you'll give me a hand, I'm going to rig that big tarpaulin lashed over the tailgate as a fly over the hood of the wagon. It's going to be hot today and I like to see a woman travel in comfort."

IV

Lavery's premonition of heat during the day seemed based on as sound a ground as Marta's premonition of serious trouble. The sun was a molten flame in a brassy bowl.

Lavery had spent $100 in minted gold pieces on the river for a map of the country he intended to cross. One of the hand-drawn and hand-lettered jobs a man could find in the Missouri towns in profusion—most of them purporting to be faithful copies of an Army survey, a few of them bearing facsimiles of the signature of a Lieutenant John Charles Frémont.

Cole had thought his better than most. It was clearly drawn and lettered and bore none of the cabalistic designs and drawings with which most of them were littered—notations of the location of the Gates of Hell, the spot where Fire River burst from the mountain and raced across the desert, and the great Ice Slide, near the summit of the divide, where wagoners could make skids for their wagons and sleds for their teams and skate at a breathless, time-saving speed.

According to Lavery's map, the course McIntyre was trying to follow from the Great Salt Lake was roughly parallel to a great river that cut in from the north and east, tearing a massive hole through the surface of the earth. Directly across their path, according to the map, was a shadowed area noted as the Devil's Sink. This was ringed with sharply marked mountains.

It was this Lavery had chiefly feared when McIntyre suggested the southward change of course. The Sierras, lying across the northern route to the Truckee and down the tributaries of the Sacramento, were high, also. But they were cool and rich with water. They had seemed the best passage. They still seemed so.

The string of wagons had formed again. Lavery's wagon had wound up on the tail of the string. Now, as Cole sat on the seat, a low, hot wind was sweeping the dust of the wheels back on his face. The wind was also whipping the tarpaulin he had rigged as a fly over the hood, and it kept snapping the ties of the hood open so that much of the dust funneled on inside the wagon where Marta was at work.

Presently she appeared at the ties of the tilt, her face red with heat and exertion and streaked with sweat. She frowned at the wagons ahead and at a distant line of black mountains stretched across the horizon.

"The wind is stronger, Cole," she said. "That isn't only dust on the wind now. It's sand. It's beginning to sting. Coming right from those mountains. And look at the teams."

Lavery had been noticing the animals ahead of him, just as he had been flinching a little from the rising bite of blown sand in the wind. His animals were among the best in the train, but they were heads down this morning, moving sluggishly and with evident uneasiness. Instinct was at work in them. The wind and the brassiness of the sky meant more than the present discomfort of sand and wind and heat.

Cole nodded agreement, and Marta sat on the seat beside him. They drove in silence for half an hour. At the end of this time the wind had risen to an ugly thing with a steady, harsh impact. Curiously the heat rose with the wind, as though the moving air was a draft from a furnace.

Still short of mid-morning, a man on horseback appeared to one side of Lavery's wagon, head down against the blast of the wind, eyes stung red by the drift of sand.

When Lavery came abreast of him, the rider pulled over and rode in alongside the box. Lavery recognized him as Uncle Bill Mann, Mrs. Wilson's father, who had been serving as a self-appointed aide to whoever was captain of the string, all the way out from Missouri. Uncle Bill leaned out of his saddle to shout at Cole.

"Something bad on the other side of those mountains ahead," he bellowed. "Wind's coming from there. Don't like it. Too damned hot. My God, but it's hot! Thought I better check back along the string and see that everybody was in place. You're the last wagon, Lavery. I'll pull up ahead."

Cole nodded. Uncle Bill reined ahead and vanished into the dust drifting back from the other wagons. A few moments later, Lavery's team came to an abrupt halt against the tailgate of the wagon ahead. This was no place or time to stop.

Lavery passed the reins to Marta and jumped down. He shoved past two or three wagons and came to the Wilson tilt. A bunch of men and women were gathered at a brush clump a little to one side of it. Uncle Bill Mann's horse was there, head hanging and saddle empty.

Cole pushed through the press. The old man was down on his back on the ground. His mouth was open. Drifting dust had already stained his teeth. His face was a deep purple. He was dead. Lavery had seen a man dead of a failed heart before, and he had looked like this. Heat had ruined more than one weak heart. Heat had killed Uncle Bill.

Mrs. Wilson was beside Cole. He turned to her with a word of sympathy on his lips, but Mrs. Wilson's eyes were on him, her stare like a blow. She did not believe heat had killed her father.

"He was back to your wagon," she said. "He said he was going to check the whole string . . . even to your rig. He was back there, just now."

"Damn it, he should have knowed better!" someone shouted. "We don't get rid of bad luck by letting it string along behind us. We get rid of it by leaving it behind. Lavery argued against this trail and he's been hoping we'd get turned back. A man pulling against everybody else makes bad luck."

Lavery turned away, neither identifying the wagon train man who was talking or waiting to hear him out. The sand in the air was chafing the tempers of everybody in the string. The sun had heated their blood. The long impatience and the minor troubles of the crossing had built to a climax. The pot was about to boil.

He didn't want to leave Marta alone now—not alone in the wagon. Maybe it was that, and maybe it was only that he wasn't sure what was coming and he wanted to be with her when it arrived. He walked swiftly back to his own wagon.

Marta did not ask questions, once she had looked at his face. Reaching into the tilt behind her, she slid out his double rifle, earing back one hammer and checking to be certain the caps were in place as he had taught her.

In a moment or two, the others came back along the string. Forsythe and Wilson and Simon and the rest, with

Bert McIntyre, red of face and angry, in the lead. McIntyre came in close to the box of the wagon, putting his thigh against the hub of the near wheel, and glared upward.

"You still against taking my short cut, Lavery?" he growled.

"I am," Cole said quietly. "The weather we've had today gives you a faint idea why. And this is only the beginning. How you going to find us a pothole of water tonight, after this drift sand has had a chance to fill all the potholes in? How you going to see where to dig for water with fresh drift to cover all surface sign? How long can the women and the kids stand this heat? Wagons can't get through this way. Not with the luck shaping up for us."

"Quit talking of luck, Lavery, for God's sake," Wilson protested. "You make it worse. Thing is, we figure you're our bad luck. It's been bad since you started bucking McIntyre and the rest of us at the turn-off. It's a hell of a thing to do, but we all got to think of our own families. We're changing our luck, right here. We're leaving you and the missus behind us. We don't want no more of you."

"And you're heading on south?" Lavery asked quietly.

Wilson nodded.

Lavery shrugged. "You're not getting away from any-thing, then," he said surely. "Your luck will stay with you as long as you keep pointed the way you are."

"As long as I captain the team, maybe?" McIntyre asked raggedly.

Lavery looked at the man's reddened, sand-stung eyes. His voice had the eerie, savage note of the wind itself. McIntyre was pulling too big a load. He was too small a man to captain a train. His own ambition for a reputation outweighed his judgment. He knew, inside, that the train should turn back, but he intended to bull ahead.

"Yes," Lavery said. "That's exactly what I mean."

"Get down!" McIntyre shouted. "Damn you, get down. I've had enough. I should have settled this days ago. This ain't the time, but it'll do. Get down, or you want me to come up there after you?"

Lavery felt Marta stir beside him, the stock of his rifle in her hands. He stood up, keeping nostrils closed against the drift in the wind, and stepped out onto the rim of the near wheel.

As he did so, a man up near the head of Lavery's team moved in close to one of the animals, intending to use its lee for shelter from the wind to light his pipe. His match flared. Lavery yelled warning, knowing the fellow was too close to a sensitive eye and ear, but he was too late. The flame blossomed and the nervous horse lunged forward, transmitting its sudden fear to its teammates. The wagon rocked sharply forward a yard, turning the wheel beneath Lavery's feet.

Cole's yell, the movement of the wagon, and his sudden spill into space might have seemed something else to a nervous, taut man below him. As he twisted, trying to avoid coming down on McIntyre, he saw the man tear the long-barreled pistol from his belt. He saw the weapon tilt upward. He saw the smoke belch from its muzzle. He felt a sharp, paralyzing prick of pain that twisted him an instant before he fell against the man.

Then, when he had spilled onto the dust and was trying to get his knees under him, he heard the heavy smash of his rifle from the seat above him.

Swaying to his knees, Lavery saw McIntyre staggering a yard away, bent nearly double, both hands clenched against a great hole in his belly. Turning, he looked up at Marta, white-faced and wild-eyed, standing behind the length of his rifle, the hammer back on its second barrel now, her lips

146

moving as she cried a warning to the other men about him.

He did not hear Marta above the roar of the wind, but a man close at hand shouted raggedly.

"She's crazy . . . wild! Let's get out of here!"

The men wheeled away. Cole tried to stagger up onto his feet, he tried to call after them—to stop them. But they were gone and there was only dust and wind and blackness. Blackness he could not avoid. He stumbled and pitched into it, thinking that he had failed utterly.

He was hit, maybe fatally, leaving Marta alone. And the wagon men were not turning back. Bert McIntyre was dead, cut down by Marta. Marta, who had never harmed any soul in her life, but who had known how to defend her husband when he was hurt and down. And the others were gone, on to the south with their impatience, ignoring the savagery of the wind and the country, leaving her with a dead man and another who might be dying.

A man tried to scheme his way around a problem. He tried to do it to save others from the results of their own mistakes, and he got this. He brought this on the wife he had married a few short weeks ago, back on the river. A trail ended like this.

There was still a wind, but the sand no longer hit at Lavery's face. He was under the tilt of his wagon. The fly he had rigged as additional sun shelter still snapped, but not so loudly as it had in the beginning of the storm. There was beard on his cheeks—maybe a three days' growth.

The hurt from McIntyre's gunshot was localized in his body now, lying between his upper ribs, drawing irritably as it began to knit, but not fevered and booming through his whole body as it had been.

Marta came in under the tilt, her eyes brightening as she

saw his own open. She knelt beside him, fussing with the blanket across his chest and concealing the rather too thorough job of bandaging she had done there. She answered his unspoken question with a nod.

"Yes, they're gone," she said quietly. "All of them. They came back and buried Mister McIntyre. They wanted us to go with them. You won, you see, Cole. You and the wind and the sand. They turned north. They waited a day, trying to persuade me to drive with them. In the end they left me, because I insisted."

"I could have stood the driving," Cole said. "You were crazy to stay behind."

"Was I, Cole?" Marta asked. "I wonder. I turned the horses loose. I found them pawing at some saw grass roots. I dug these and found water almost on the surface. You were resting well. A drive would not have been good for you. And Cole, what if there is a short cut across through here? Wouldn't it be a good thing to find?"

This was different than McIntyre's hunger to make a name for himself as a guide. Marta was thinking of shortened distance and easier traveling, not for herself, but for wheels that might follow. He stared at her, wondering how many years it took a man to know the woman he had married. Marta Lavery—who had sung for her passage on a riverboat and had married an admittedly greenhorned wagon man—had already killed a man. Now she talked of crossing a desert no man knew. And she meant what she was talking about.

"The air has cleared since the storm, Cole," she said. "In the early morning I can see mountains a little south and west of us with snow on them. And there's a line of ridges that look greener than the rest of this country. California can't be too far beyond the mountains. The stock is in good shape. And one wagon could make a dangerous crossing where a train might have real trouble. If we weren't impatient, and if we took it easy. . . ." Marta shrugged, smiling. "I don't know why I'm asking you, even, except we're a partnership. Until you're on your feet, at least, I'm boss of this party. The others have gotten so far to the north now we could never overtake them, and, if we're going to travel alone, why not fill in some of the blanks on that map of ours?"

"We can't ask for the kind of luck we'd need," Cole said in protest.

Marta laughed at him. "Us ask for luck?" she mocked. "Why? You made the bad luck that turned the wagons with us back to the north. Just whoop up some good luck for us. That's all we'll need. Luck runs that way, anyhow, I think. It's made, rather than found. Cole, I want to make our own road to the Pacific."

The country was in Marta's blood as it was in his, then. Time was the thing they had. Out of time and a little courage and a bright hopefulness, anything could be built. Even a southern highway to the Pacific. Cole worked himself upright on his cot in the wagon bed and made himself comfortable.

"Hand me the map, then. Let's figure out near as we can where we are. Tomorrow we'll load our kegs with water and make some medicine for luck, and we'll see how close we can get to those snowy mountains of yours."

Marta bent and kissed him, and Cole Lavery thought that he could have been mistaken, right from the beginning— maybe the southern road to the Californias was as good as any other, after all. There was one certain sure way for a man to find out.

The Curse of San Stefan

The author sent the fifth and last Cole Lavery story to his
agent on September 17, 1948. He titled it "The Curse of
San Stefan". It was submitted to Mike Tilden at Popular
Publications who had a slot for a story of 7,500 words in
New Western. Tilden asked Blackburn to cut the story from
8,250 words to 7,500 words on October 5, 1948. The cut
version was submitted on October 21, 1948. Mike Tilden
bought the story on December 9, 1948 for $150, paying 2¢
a word. It was retitled "They'll Never Take Our Land"
when it appeared in *New Western* (3/49). For its appearance
here the author's carbon of his original typescript has been
used and his title has been restored.

I

Marta pressed in a little more closely to Cole—perhaps a
woman's instinctive appeal to her husband in time of
trouble. With his eyes on the group riding up to their encamped wagon, Lavery disengaged his wife's hands.

"Stay here," he told her quietly.

Marta's back stiffened. "No. I've been beside you all
the way from Missouri. Now we're at last on our own
land . . . our piece of California . . . our own beginning. I

150

belong beside you more than ever."

Lavery frowned and started toward the encamped wagon, from which Marta and he had walked a short distance several moments before. As he moved, he uneasily eyed the men dismounting there. This southern piece of California was troubled country. A friendly party did not approach a camp so boldly as this. Men were jumpy. Violence was close to the surface. Ruthlessness was the stock in trade of many.

The dismounted men at the wagon ignored Lavery's approach. One took up an axe and went to work on the spokes of one wagon wheel. Another tumbled a sack of flour from the wagon and slit it end to end with one stroke of a broadbladed knife. A third kicked over Marta's bright little cast-iron stove, his heavy, iron-capped boots shattering the castings like glass.

The man at the wagon wheel stepped back. The wheel collapsed. The wagon tilted crazily. Marta's trunk, shaken loose from its place inside, tumbled out onto the ground, spilling its contents.

Lavery made no outcry. He was too wise for this. But such an anger as he had never known shook him. He moved up steadily, stopping to face one man of the raiding party who stood a little apart from the others. He was obviously their leader. The man, wearing a belted gun, stood at ease and watched the destruction his fellows were working with bland satisfaction. He was a handsome man, well dressed, a little florid, and as Yankee as a silver dollar.

Lavery spoke quietly to him, the heat of his anger forging his voice to a fine hot edge.

"If you're looking for a short road to hell, mister, you've sure found it. I promise you that."

The man spat carefully with the wind. "You're squatting

on private grass . . . a piece of my ranch."

"I've got a deed to it, signed by the governor," Lavery protested.

"A Mexican deed," the man snorted. "Not worth the paper it's written on. The only valid titles in this country are American, written on good old United States paper and signed with Yankee names. That's the kind I'm going to have to all the land on this bench . . . twenty miles of it. No Mexican deed squatters are going to cloud my title before I've got U.S. papers on it. This is a rancher's country. You've had your warning. We've left you your horses. Now, get off this grass and stay off it!"

Lavery stared at the man, bitter with impotence, clinging to the knowledge there was at this moment nothing he could do, knowing that to control his anger was to save his life. Marta straightened beside him and spoke in a cool, unhurried voice.

"Maybe you didn't understand my husband. This is our land. Supposing you and your dirty-necked coyotes take your own advice."

The tall man took a sudden angry step forward. "I've wasted enough time with you mule-heads. And I don't take lip from any woman."

Lavery made his protest then, forcing it through the tight wall with which he contained his livid fury. "My wife's condition is delicate. Do your business with me, mister."

"Are you going to start moving . . . now?" the man asked.

Lavery looked at Marta. Her head was still high. She answered. "We'll be here when you and every man like you in California has been hanged!" she said with a savage conviction.

The man stabbed his finger at Lavery. "All right, I'll do

my business with you, squatter. It takes a Yankee to take the stubbornness out of a stubborn Yankee and I know how it's done. Spread him out against a wagon wheel, boys, and a couple of you keep this witch turned so that she can see Cy McGann plays for keeps!"

Grass was cool beneath Lavery's naked, ribboned back. A high midnight moon shone in his eyes. Pain tore at every fiber of his body. He had a moment of dull shame—the shame of a strong man who has collapsed before an enemy and before the woman he loves. This passed swiftly and Lavery felt only the tremendous tide of his anger and the desire to move. He sat up.

Marta sat a scant pair of yards away from him, leaning awkwardly against the side of her overturned trunk, her chin on her breast. He could not tell if she was sleeping or not. Fear knifed through him—the only real fear he believed he would ever know again—fear for her.

This had been their land, bought with money carefully hoarded. This had been their place under the sun, the sod in which their roots would anchor. This had been their first night upon that land.

Marta had seen her sunset happiness shattered. She had felt the touch of violent hands upon her. She had seen further violence done Cole himself. Certainly it had been Marta who had cut him down from the wagon wheel to which he had been lashed after the departure of Cy McGann and his men. It had been Marta who had rubbed his stripped back with ointment and had rolled him onto the coolness of the grass. It had been Marta, stirring in the darkness, who had brought some order out of the chaos of the ruined camp.

She was expecting her child in the spring and such

shocks as these were dangerous for a woman in her condition. Crawling because the distance was short, Lavery reached her side and anxiously gripped her shoulders.

"Marta," he said with soft intensity.

She trembled slightly and raised her head. She had been sleeping, after all. "Cole, they hurt you so."

"The hurts are where even you can't see them," Cole told her grimly.

"We had something so wonderful here tonight," Marta breathed. "Now we're left with nothing."

"We haven't lost so much, girl," Cole said. "There's still the two of us . . . and the land. What's a wagon and a stove and a trunk full of clothes?"

"But there's nothing we can do . . . ," Marta protested.

Lavery's grip on her shoulders tightened. "That's what McGann thinks. But he's wrong, Marta. At supper tonight no one owed us anything and we had no capital for a start here. Now it's different. When we've collected what this McGann and his boys owe us for damages here, maybe our beginning will be better than we hoped, after all. I'll get you blankets from the wagon now. In the morning we'll ride back to the mission at San Juan Capistrano. I'll have to leave you there for a few days. The *padres* will take care of you."

It hurt Lavery to say this. It hurt Marta to hear it. But a man in a raw country had to be practical. So did a woman.

"Yes, Cole," Marta answered softly.

II

Mission San Juan Capistrano lay in the widest part of the valley of San Juan Creek, about three miles from the ocean.

Below it was a village and there was a clustering of shacks at tidewater where a casual lightering business in hides was done whenever a Yankee trading ship anchored off the mouth of the creek.

Between the northern outposts of San Gabriel and Pueblo Los Angeles and the old first city of California at San Diego de Alcala, San Juan was the only stopping place of importance along the Camino Real—the mission highway paralleling the coast.

An hour after sunrise, before the sleepy village in the valley roused, Cole and Marta Lavery knocked at the mission. A kindly and courteous Father Superior listened to their troubles and willingly agreed to look after Cole's wife in his absence.

"It's hard to understand your countrymen," the *padre* told Lavery. "We've seen many recently. Hard and greedy men. There have been other cases like this you report . . . people of my own race, driven from land to which they hold titles issued by the old government. We're a long way from the gold fields here and it seems a strange place to find greed."

"You know this Cy McGann, then," Lavery said. "What's he after?"

"He's driven everyone from a twenty-mile strip of the coastal grass to the south. Apparently he intends to keep it clear of settlement until the Federal Land Commission of the new government gets around to studying this part of the territory. When it does, he'll probably put in a spurious claim to the land he's chosen and try to make it stick. If there are no other settlers on it, I think he'll be successful. To cover up his real purpose, he can stir serious trouble here in the south. There are hotheads among my people who hate the Yankee government only because it is new."

"It sounds like a case for the authorities," Lavery said sharply.

The old *padre* smiled wearily. "What authorities? We had first a government by my own religious order . . . missionaries pushing into a wilderness. Then that of a Republican Mexico, too troubled at home to worry about a distant province. Now the Yankee flag. There is no authority in the south of California, *Señor* Lavery, except that of the sword and that of the fist."

Lavery rose from the bench on which he had been sitting. "I want two things from you, Father. A list of every little titleholder who has been driven off the grass along this stretch of the coast. And I want to know where I can find this Cy McGann."

"There's a place called Smuggler's Cove, some miles down the coast from your tract of San Stefan," the old priest said. "It's been used by the lawless since the first trading ships reached these waters. McGann will be there, I think. Look, we were about to sit down to breakfast when you knocked at the gate. If you and *Señora* Lavery will join us, I'll have a clerk make up the list you require while we eat."

Lavery nodded agreement. Marta and he joined the mission brothers at their meal. At its end a clerk brought the Father Superior the list Cole had requested. The *padre* handed it to Cole.

"I give you this for one reason, my son," he said. "You will find good friends among these names if you seek them."

"That isn't why I asked for it," Cole told him bluntly.

The old man smiled. "I didn't ask your reasons," he murmured. "I'm merely giving you a reason that's acceptable to me. Have you forgotten that it is written . . . vengeance is the Lord's?"

"No," Cole said. He folded the list and put it into the pocket of his shirt. As an afterthought, he produced the deed that gave Marta and himself title to San Stefan *rancho.*

"I'd appreciate it if you'd keep this for a while."

The Father Superior nodded, took the deed, and turned toward his cell. Marta walked with Cole to the mission gate. "Three days, Cole. I can stand not hearing from you . . . not seeing you . . . for only three days. If you're not back by then, I'll start out to look for you."

Cole kissed her. "You and the *padre*. He says no revenge, and you expect a miracle in three days. It's all right. If I can't do what I have to in three days, thirty years couldn't be enough time. We'll have supper two nights from tonight . . . together."

Marta clung to him for a moment, then let him go in silence.

Moving from San Juan across the grass of San Stefan and on to the southward in the direction of Smuggler's Cove, Lavery studied the country. Now, since he was struggling for ownership of a portion of it, he saw it with different eyes. Unlike so much of the interior valley country of California that he had seen, this coastal bench was rich in its own right, not requiring water to turn it green. Ocean fogs, rolling in even in dry season, accounted for this. It was not a planter's country. There was not enough water for this. But it was a cattleman's paradise. It was easy to understand why Cy McGann wanted this particular twenty miles.

The business of California ranchers had always been in cattle—poor and scrubby creatures whose greatest asset was that they had skin upon their backs. All California beef was raised for hides and tallow alone. The carcasses were given to the incredibly poor Indians of the inland hills or left to rot in the sun when they were skinned out.

Lavery saw a different kind of operation, the same thing that McGann must also see. At one time 100 ships called off of San Diego and Pueblo Los Angeles where now one called. And one time soon, gold-seekers from the north, weary of trying to win fortunes by luck, would drift southward by the thousands into this more pleasant land. They would again think of the trades and farms at which they had worked in the East before gold hysteria had brought them across the country.

Beef herds, raised for beef instead of for hides, and carefully built up through the years could produce fortunes when a new and growing country began to clamor for more food than it had ever needed before. It was for this reason that Marta and he wished to build here. McGann must have a similar wish. Otherwise, this bench would have no value to him.

As he rode south, Lavery reviewed his own position. The seizure of the California government from the dying Mexican rule in 1846 had foreshadowed quarrels and contests over land claims that were flooding the commission set up to study and settle them in the north. A great many of those who held old titles to unimproved land upon which they couldn't prove occupancy were hastily selling them off for whatever price they could get.

San Stefan, 10,000 acres of the most beautiful grassland Cole had ever seen, had cost Marta and himself a little less than $3,000 in American cash. The old man who sold it to them, a descendant of the original grantee, had been honest enough to tell them that they might find their title hard to prove and harder to hold. A man gained nothing without risk, and there was only one other way to secure land here. McGann's way.

It was possible that McGann was thinking even beyond the value of the land itself. It was possible that he was aware his plan would give him twenty miles of country through which the Camino Real passed—the one land route from San Diego to Los Angeles. The pressures he could put on whoever traveled that road were many and varied.

It was the old story of one man taking from others for his own profit. Lavery realized that a man less direct than he was might have spent months trying to obtain official sanction and the help of others who had been similarly injured. A less direct man might have devised an intricate plot to defeat McGann. However, it was in Lavery's blood to be as direct as a bullet in flight. To Cole the obvious course was to invoke McGann's own thinking against him—to take from him as he was attempting to take from others.

Stiffened by a long ride on his awkward-gaited wagon horse and from the drying scars of the thorough rope's-end lashing he had taken against his own wagon wheel the night before, Lavery dismounted late in the afternoon some distance up the little dry creek running into the sea at Smuggler's Cove.

III

The outlaw hang-out was a brief collection of brush shacks, a short wooden street, and a small boat landing, protected from the surge of the open sea by a tongue of rock and from the openness of the bench country behind it by a steep arroyo. Lying on his belly on the brink of the bluff above the water, Lavery studied the settlement below for some time. A small, dirty, well-weathered ship rode her hawsers some distance off shore. A ship's small

159

boat was nosed into the sand below the settlement.

Above this, safely beyond high water mark, rose an untidy stack of barrels, hogsheads, crates, and packing cases. The sand between this careless pile and the water's edge was torn up by the feet of many men. Lavery judged that these were supplies or merchandise of some kind that had been landed from the ship. However, he was puzzled by the fact that the seamen who must have rowed the small boat ashore were nowhere in sight about the settlement.

There were, however, a number of idling Yankees moving along the boardwalk before the seaward-facing huts of the town. Among them Lavery recognized at least two of those who had broken up the camp Marta and he had established on San Stefan. Satisfied that this was the headquarters McGann was using, Lavery withdrew from the bluff to wait the coming of darkness, using the intervening time to study in detail the steeply slanting arroyo that gave land access to the settlement. By the time the sun had briefly silhouetted the ugly, bluff-bowed little ship and had dropped on behind the horizon, Lavery had memorized every inch of the descending arroyo and the set-up of Smuggler's Cove.

He was disconcerted when, with lowering darkness, Cy McGann issued from one of the shacks and detailed two men who took up guard positions at the bottom of the land entrance. Lavery had no choice now but to start along the rim of the bluff until he could find another arroyo that would drop him to the water's edge.

He walked nearly two miles before he found a suitable place, and once on the sand he worked back up the beach. He was well within earshot of the uproar of drinking men, when he heard a small party working along the sand toward him. Pressing in among some rocks at the base of the bluff, he waited.

The tide was low. In the faint remaining afterglow of sunset he made out four men. Among them were two he recognized as a portion of the raiding party at San Stefan. They were alternately dragging and kicking a fifth man along through the sand.

Abreast of Lavery they turned down across the black, slippery rocks exposed by the receding tide, dragging their prisoner with them. They worked with unhurried callousness, fastening the man in a spread-eagle on a particularly nasty pile of rocks far below the high-tide line. Leaving him there, they turned back toward the shacks of the cove.

When they were gone, Lavery moved down to the rocks, taking care to walk only on exposed crags and to keep the prints of his boots out of the wet sand. The man pinioned on the rocks was of middle age, graying somewhat, and he was dressed in blue seaman's clothing of good material and cut. It had been badly torn and misused, apparently in struggles with his captors. The man had been mercilessly mauled about the head and face and lay quietly without moving.

Lavery was about to approach when a sound up the beach drew his attention. He moved back to the rocks at the base of the bluff. A man came unhurriedly down along the sand, found a rock to his liking, and sat down upon it. It was obvious he had been detailed to keep an eye on the man spread-eagled on the rocks.

Lavery moved soundlessly and with an increasing rush down across the sand, launching himself in the last ten feet in a flying leap. His body struck the man at the shoulder and carried him forward onto the sand.

The fellow twisted in a startled frenzy, trying to reach his gun. Lavery pinned the gun, tore it from his hand, and kicked it aside, coming to his feet. The man on the sand also bounded up, opening his mouth to shout alarm. Lavery hit him hard in the center of his face, silencing the sound.

The man pawed at Cole to keep him away and tried to shout again. Lavery went quietly and efficiently to work. The tangle lasted perhaps a minute and a half. No longer. Lavery had much work to do and little time in which to do it. The man before him broke completely after this brief run of seconds, unable to withstand the terrible mauling of Lavery's hands. He sagged heavily and soundlessly into the sand, unconscious.

In driving a blow to the man's mid-section, Lavery had bruised his hand against a money belt there. He ripped open the shirt and stripped the belt away. It was heavy but gave off no metallic sound. Cole understood. It was loaded with dust, rather than mined or minted metal—dust from the creeks to the north. There was a small fortune in the pockets of this belt.

Lifting the tail of his own shirt, Lavery strapped the belt on and tucked the shirt back in over it. He stripped the man's gun belt and buckled it about his own hips. He recovered the weapon he had earlier kicked aside and meticulously cleaned the sand from it. Then he lifted the unconscious Yankee and carried him down across the rocks to the place where the man in seaman's clothing lay spread-eagled.

The rocks on which the seaman lay were filled with barnacled crevices. The man's feet and wrists had been kicked down into these barbed crevices so that they were firmly wedged. In his condition the man could not break free. Returning tide was certain to submerge him.

Working swiftly, inwardly wincing at the damage he was forced to do the man's already lacerated feet and arms, Lavery loosened the spread-eagled seaman and lifted him clear. Having done this, he spilled the body of the guard into the same position and forced his boots and wrists down into the same crevices.

Carrying the seaman back to a more comfortable place at the base of the bluff, Lavery wet his own kerchief with sea water from a pool and carefully cleansed the man's battered face and his torn wrists and ankles. He hunkered beside the man with grim satisfaction, his eyes on the strip of beach lying between his present position and the shacks of Smuggler's Cove. He thought he had stripped the table of stakes in the first round of the game, and that he would be able to wipe the second clean before McGann even realized he had an opponent.

A few minutes after midnight, at the usual time for guard replacing, a second man came down along the sand from the noisy shacks of the settlement. He was whistling and un-hurried, apparently warmed by his own share of the drinking that had been going on among the brush huts up the beach. As he neared the place where the seaman had been stretched out on the rocks, he paused uncertainly as though in search of the first guard—the man who he was to relieve.

Lavery rose from behind the rock he had been using for a shelter and made an unintelligible grunting sound. The guard swung with relief toward him. Lavery moved swiftly forward, his gun out.

"Quiet and careful," he snapped.

The relief guard grunted astonishment and alarm but the gun in Lavery's hand was compelling. Unwilling to have the man either see his face or recognize it, Cole snapped another command: "Turn around."

The guard did so unwillingly. Cole stepped up behind him and lifted his gun from its holster, determining as he did so that this man, also, wore a heavy money belt. "Shed your dust, too," he ordered.

The man hesitated for a moment, then wheeled desperately. Cole jerked the muzzle of the gun in his hand upward in a long arc. The barrel struck flushly along the line of the man's jaw. He turned and he fell like an undercut tree. Cole slid the money belt under his shirt, and carefully propped the man's body in a somnolent upright position against the rock.

Satisfied that the appearance here was now casually that of one man on guard over another lying out on the rocks near the water's edge, Lavery retreated to where he had left the injured seaman. The man had regained consciousness. He eyed Lavery warily. Cole spoke shortly to him.

"Can you walk?"

The seaman nodded, speaking with difficulty. "All the way to hell, if it means getting out of here."

"Not that far," Cole told him. "Just to a place where we can hole up. We've got a lot of work to do here yet. Whose ship is that off shore?"

"Mine. Or was, till I came ashore. I'm Captain Enos Hale. Who the devil are you?"

"A gent Cy McGann pushed an inch too far," Cole answered. "Lavery is the name. How'd you get on McGann's blacklist? I thought what he wanted was ashore. What's a ship got to do with his plans?"

"I've done business here at this cove with one man or another in past seasons," Captain Hale said. "Called this time at the roadstead off Los Angeles to see if I couldn't make a top-price deal for my cargo of merchandise. A man brought me word, if I'd slip down here so the buyer could avoid territorial customs charges on my stuff, I could get the deal I wanted. Kind of smuggling, but always sound business before the revolt. Mexican customs tariffs almost put us traders out of business and most of us learned how to get around port authorities."

"McGann was your buyer?"

Captain Hale nodded. "Agreeable as hell, too. Had his men do all the lightering of my cargo ashore so my boys wouldn't even have to leave the ship. I wouldn't have any crew ashore when he threw the hooks to me. When the stuff was stacked on the beach, I came after my money. When I landed, he grabbed me. Told me that since I'd smuggled the stuff ashore and had no recourse with the authorities because of that, he wasn't going to pay me a red cent. When I'd agree to order my ship south to San Diego, he'd send me south along the coast to rejoin her there."

"You told him . . . ?"

"To go to hell!" the captain answered with spirit. "He's no usual half-smuggler, half-pirate. He's got something else up his sleeve. He and his men have got a fortune in gold among them. Carry it in belts on them. Brought it down from the north. Probably panned it out of the creeks up there at gunpoint. He could have paid me but wouldn't. That doesn't go with Enos Hale."

"So he spread you out to drown."

"Or break down and give in. It would have worked, if you hadn't come along. My boys on the *Queen* know something's wrong, but they only work for pay and they've got to think of the ship. They wouldn't risk coming in against McGann's outfit. They'd wait a while, then up anchor and pray for a running wind. So it was give in or die for me."

IV

Lavery considered Captain Hale's story. Trade goods set ashore here meant McGann had some use for them. Cole had not figured McGann as a trader. He said so. The captain of the *Queen* shifted position painfully.

"This country's been asleep for years," he said. "It's just coming alive. It needs everything. That's what a trader's cargo is, these days . . . everything. I'd rather be ashore here with a load of trade goods than I would to have the best claim in the Mother Lode. There'd be more profit from it in the long run. McGann knows that. Does it make sense to you, Lavery?"

Cole nodded. If McGann had twenty miles of this coast to control and could establish himself as a trader for the whole area, too, the growth of the country would bring him wealth a man couldn't measure.

"McGann's working at gunpoint where he can," Enos Hale went on, "but, if he gets in a tight, he can buy himself out of it, too. He and his boys are loaded with dust. Got an iron safe of it in McGann's shack at the cove, besides what he and the rest are carrying on them."

Lavery stood up. "That's what interests me . . . their dust."

"And their blood," Hale growled. "Me, too, Lavery. Supposing me and you go partners in this business you claim you've got ahead of you?"

Lavery studied the man for a moment, then handed him the gun he had taken from the second guard. Hale balanced it in his lacerated hand with a surprising show of skill. He grinned widely.

"Counting McGann and checking off those two down there on the rocks that you've put out of business," he said with relish, "there's eight men left at the cove. And there's two of us. Right interesting odds. Where we going to start?"

Lavery thought of the careful study he had made of the layout of the cove and the arroyo.

"At the top," he said, and he pointed to the rim of the sea bluff above them.

There was sand in Enos Hale. All movement was painful for him, but he rose and followed Lavery gamely down the beach to the arroyo. He climbed up through this to the bench above without complaint. They moved back along the bench to a position on the bluff directly over the huddled shacks of Smuggler's Cove. The two of them hunkered down. Presently three or four men, one of them carrying a lantern, emerged from a shack and started along the beach in the direction of the rocks on which Enos Hale had been wedged.

The captain eyed them with concern. "They're going to find out what's happened down there in a couple of minutes. They're going to find out you've taken a bite out of their backside. And McGann isn't a boy that'll stand still. What do we do then?"

"Take another bite," Lavery said bluntly.

The lantern bobbed far down the bench and halted. A moment later a man came running back, laboring in the soft sand. He began to shout as he neared the settlement. Doors burst open. Several men came out onto the rickety boardwalk that served as a street. One of them was Cy McGann.

The man from down the beach spoke hurriedly. McGann barked orders and the whole group started back along the beach. Lavery chuckled. He turned to Hale.

"Begin to see where we set our teeth next?"

Hale nodded. "Sure. You've been hurt and I haven't been paid for the goods I landed. The answer to that is the dust in McGann's safe. But how do you get to it, boy? I sure as hell can't climb up and down this cliff."

"No," Lavery agreed. "You stay here. I know the way down. I took pains to study it earlier. Night light is bad and it's a long way for sure range with a handgun. It'll be up to you to keep them off my back if they double back up the beach. What shack is the safe in?"

Hale pointed out the shelter from which Cy McGann had emerged, but he was frowning. "I got knocked down and fell against that chunk of gold-lined iron. I got a good look at it. You won't get into it with your teeth. Now, if there was a way to get word to my boys on the *Queen*, maybe I could talk them into coming ashore and lending a hand."

"Not enough time," Lavery said shortly. "Can't afford it. No way to get a message out, anyway. We'll move over to the head of the arroyo leading down into the cove. You'll stay at the top with all our spare ammunition. I'm going to empty that safe."

Enos Hale whistled admiration and perhaps disbelief, but said nothing further, stiffly rising to follow as Lavery moved toward the head of the arroyo. They trooped on single file.

Lavery felt satisfaction in his own ability at memorization. He moved down the slanting, uncertain footpath leading to the beach at Smuggler's Cove with ease, each twist and bad spot turning up as he thought it should. Darkness lay against the sea bluff. He could not tell how long McGann and his men would be absent down the beach, examining the prints Enos Hale and he had left as partial explanation of what had happened to the guards at the water's edge.

Reaching the bottom of the footpath, Lavery moved along the rickety wooden walk between the huddled shanties, his eyes darting into the shadows. Presently he saw what he wanted—a rusty bar of iron, one end of which had been hammered flat for use as a lever. With this in his hand, he turned into Cy McGann's shack. The place was an arsenal.

He had no difficulty locating the safe of which Enos Hale had spoken. With sight of it came a surge of elation.

Strongboxes were being manufactured in an increasing variety of makes and kinds, some of them too stout for any but the most skillful breakers. This, however, was an old cast-iron box with a corroded nickel combination dial and a trip-lever against the opening side of the door. Lavery had seen one opened with a great deal of weight and violence.

Careless now of sound, with haste his prime objective, Lavery rammed the flattened end of the lever bar behind the lip of the combination dial and brought steady pressure to bear. The pressure increased slowly as he leaned his weight against it. The metal gave just a little, protesting rustily.

Outside, a handgun banged on the crest of the bluff and shouting surged up, startled and loud.

V

Lavery knew there was no hurrying the job on his hands now. With luck the pressure he was bringing against the combination dial of the safe might snap the key blades of the lock and draw the whole mechanism out of the safe door. But too sharp a strain might snap the combination shaft before the lock itself pulled.

He heard running feet hit the far end of the wooden walk. The gun on the bluff, fired with cool unhurriedness by Enos Hale, snapped twice more, then fell silent. Men below answered the fire. The steel against which Cole was prying still continued to protest the strain but did not give. More shots sounded outside.

Suddenly, when his attention was on these exterior sounds, when he was measuring the seconds left before he would have to abandon the safe and sprint for the arroyo path and safety, the safe rocked and the combination dial and lock pulled out. Protesting steel screamed loudly in the shack.

At the other end of the walk a man barked sharp inquiry, then roared an order, apparently stirred by the sound. Lavery thrust two fingers in the hole left in the safe door by the pulled lock assembly and depressed the pawls that held the locking bar of the door. The bar itself, however, seemed rusted too much to move with the small leverage his fingers could manage.

A man's boots beat on the walk outside. With the fingers of one hand still thrust into the hole in the safe door, Lavery turned and fired his gun at a silhouette appearing in the shack doorway.

He only brushed the man. The fellow yelped and ran back along the walk. Suddenly the locking bar of the safe door *clicked* and the door swung open. A fat row of buckskin bags sat on the safe floor. Cole scooped them into his shirt and ducked out onto the walk, moving awkwardly with the fresh, heavy burden against his belly. Enos Hale was firing again from the bluff, but Cy McGann was shrewd.

The tracks Cole and Enos Hale had left on the sand down the beach had betrayed the fact that there were only two of them. Realizing this and hearing Hale firing from above, McGann had driven his men to separate the two who were making this attack against him. Rather than rush the shack, McGann had wedged his crew into a pocket under the bluff at the foot of the arroyo pathway.

With the men in this position, Hale could not reach them from above. Cole himself could not make his way back up the arroyo. McGann would wait for better light and then flush him out from among the shacks. Lavery swore silently.

The mauled and lacerated ship captain on the bluff above was not this easily cheated of revenge. There was a wink of light from above, then a fiercely burning greasewood root came sailing out and down. It landed on the thatched brush roof of a shack some distance from Lavery.

A man in McGann's crew broke cover and started climbing up to shake the fire brand free. Lavery dropped to one knee, aimed carefully, and rolled the fellow from the roof to the ground. Lavery leaped far to one side as he shot to avoid any return fire. Half a dozen guns banged at the muzzle flash and one marksman almost guessed his leap correctly, slamming a bullet through his now bulging shirt.

McGann's voice rose angrily: "Get that fire out!"

It was a useless command. The dry brush of the roof was already burning fiercely, throwing a widening halo of light over the cove. Nevertheless, two men did try to snuff the flames, only to be checked as Enos Hale threw gunfire at them from above.

McGann's voice bellowed another order: "Leave the one down here! He can't slip away unless he can swim. Get up the trail and flush that devil off the bluff . . . all of you!"

There was a concerted rush for the foot of the arroyo. Lavery rose from the place where he had been crouching and sprinted heavily for the trail. Hale could hold back two or maybe three men, but not the whole force. The seaman was so crippled by the injuries he had suffered at the hands of these men that he couldn't retreat from them.

This was the close fighting he had wanted to avoid. Lavery had to give Hale some diversion under which he could fall back to a safer place. He heard men scrambling up the steep slope ahead of him as he reached the foot of the bluff, but this, also, was apparently a trap McGann had set. A figure suddenly appeared before him, stepping out of shadows among the rocks. A gun flamed almost in his face. He felt a savage, spinning blow in his mid-section and went down under it.

McGann's voice rang out triumphantly: "One down!"

The man jumped forward then, his foot swinging for a merciless kick at Lavery's prostrate figure. Snagging out one hand as he rolled to avoid the blow, Lavery caught the man's boot and tugged hard on it. McGann lost his balance and spilled down.

Lavery reached his knees just as McGann rolled his gun clear. Cole was hurried and made a messy shot but McGann's face vanished in a welter of ruin, even as Lavery steadied his gun for a second shot.

Aware of a rent in his shirt and something spilling from it, Lavery realized McGann's bullet had lodged in one of the pouches of gold dust, taking his wind with the impact, but doing no other injury. He started scrambling up the arroyo path after McGann's climbing men, only to realize suddenly that there was silence at the upper end—not even the sound of movement.

Puzzled, he straightened cautiously at the top of the path. McGann's men were there. So, also, was Enos Hale, grinning as he walked under upraised hands to strip from each the money belt he wore. And beyond Hale and McGann's men other figures were indistinct in the darkness. All but one.

"Marta!" Cole grunted, recognizing her instantly.

She ran to him, grabbing her arms excitedly about the pouch-thickened bulge of his shirt. "Cole, you didn't really think I could wait for three days, did you? Not when you were in danger!"

Lavery saw then the bright, smiling Spanish faces of the

men behind her—men wearing rich togs and poor. Men with a traditional racial enjoyment in the tokens of affection exchanged between a man and his woman.

"I made the Father Superior tell me where I could find our neighbors on either side of San Stefan . . . the ones McGann ran off ahead of us," Marta hurried on. "We all came together to help you take care of a neighborhood problem. Cole, what on earth have you got tucked away inside your shirt?"

"Gold," Lavery said. "Enough to pay us . . . and these neighbors of ours, Marta . . . for the damages they suffered at McGann's hands. Enough to pay Captain Hale here for the goods he landed and the beating he took. Some left over for the Father Superior and the Mission San Juan, I think."

Enos Hale limped over to stand beside Lavery and his wife. He eyed them both with speculation. "I've got an idea," he said. "You two aim to ranch here. Ain't no doubt you'll hold onto title to your land now. I'm after long-term profits, rather than just quick and small ones. Supposing I consign my goods to you. You seem to be in good with your neighbors. They're going to have to build, same as you. They'll need supplies. And there ought to be trade along the Camino Real, passing your place. Supposing the Laverys, ma'am and mister, go into partnership with me. I stock the place. You build the store. We'll split what we make. How does that kind of a deal sound to you? I got a notion I'd like to retire here when I'm done with the sea, and that'd be a nice business to have a piece of. Supposing you give my gold to the *padre,* too, and then you can go into business with me."

Marta looked at Lavery. He frowned. "I've got my hands full, Hale. I wish I could, but I have too much to do."

"But I haven't," Marta cut in. "That's just it. While

you're building up San Stefan, I can be building the store and making friends. Please, Cole, let that be my job. I didn't come out here to take a rest cure."

"Looks like you've got yourself some partners, Captain Hale," Lavery said with a wry grin. The seaman chuckled with satisfaction and turned to look at the country behind them, coming now into focus in the increasing dawn light.

"Beautiful," he said. "Hard to figure why there'd have to be so much trouble over it. Hope that's done with. It's time for it to grow."

"Yes," Marta agreed. "It is beautiful, Captain. Almost too beautiful. We've a great deal of work to do. It will take a big country to hold all the people that will come here." Marta turned toward Cole then, smiling widely. "Our neighbors stopped to right our wagon at San Stefan, Cole. We spent our first night of ownership on our ranch. I'd like to spend a little of the second there, too. Captain Hale and our neighbors can come along behind us and be our guests. We'll have breakfast together and then a celebration . . . a real *fiesta* . . . on Mister McGann."

About the Author

Tom W. Blackburn was born on the T.O. Ranch near Raton, New Mexico. The T.O. controlled such a vast domain it had its own internal railroad system and was later used as the setting for Blackburn's novel, *Raton Pass* (1950). Blackburn first began writing Western stories for pulp magazines and, in the decade from 1938 to 1948, he contributed over 300 stories of varying lengths to such outstanding magazines as *Dime Western, Lariat Story Magazine, Western Story,* and *Star Western.* Also during the 1940s he worked as a screenwriter for various Hollywood studios, a circumstance that prepared him to adapt his own Western novels into screenplays, beginning with his first, *Short Grass* (1947). Blackburn's longest affiliation was with the Disney studio where, for a time, he was best known for having written the lyrics for "The Ballad of Davy Crockett," a popular television and then theatrical series based on the exploits of this legendary frontiersman. In his Western novels, Blackburn tended toward stories based on historical episodes, such as *Navajo Canyon* (1952) and *A Good Day to Die* (1967). Perhaps his finest achievement as a novelist is the five-part Stanton saga focused on the building of a great ranch in New Mexico from the Spanish period to the end of the 19th century. Following a stroke, Blackburn came to spend the years prior to his death in 1992 living with his daughter Stephanie in Colorado, surrounded by the mountains he had always loved. Tom W. Blackburn's Western fiction is concerned with the struggles, torments, joys, and the rare warmth that comes from companionships of the soul, the very stuff which is as imperishable in its human significance as the "sun-dark skins of the clean blood of the land" which he celebrated and transfixed in shimmering images and unforgettable characters. *The Treasure of San Felice* will be his next **Five Star Western**.